Bofuri

IZ

Iz's STATS

Lv52
HP 100/100
MP 100/100
[STR 45]
[VIT 20]
[AGI 80]
[DEX 210]
[INT 50]

Welcome
NewWor

"And the finishing touch!"

If the two of them worked together, nothing could stand in their way.

MAPLE
The strongest guild master. Takes no damage.

During the seventh event

Skills

Strike, Crafting Mastery X, Crafting Secrets II,
Enhance Success Rate Boost (L), Gathering Speed Boost (L),
Mining Speed Boost (L), Affection II, Sneaky Steps III,
Smithing X, Sewing X, Horticulture X, Synthesizing X,
Augmentation X, Cooking X, Mining X, Gathering X,
Swimming IV, Diving V, Shearing, Godsmith's Grace X

IZ'S STATS

Iz		
Lv52	HP 100/100	MP 100/100
[STR 45]	[VIT 20]	
[AGI 60]	[DEX 200]	[INT 50]

Bofuri

★ I Don't ★
Want to Get
Hurt, so I'll
⑥ Max Out My
Defense.

YUUMIKAN

Illustration by KOIN

YEN ON
NEW YORK

Welcome to
NewWorld Online.

YUUMIKAN

Translation by Andrew Cunningham • Cover art by Koin

ITAINO WA IYA NANODE BOGYORYOKU NI KYOKUFURI SHITAITO OMOIMASU. Vol. 6
©Yuumikan, Koin 2019
First published in Japan in 2019 by KADOKAWA CORPORATION, Tokyo.
English translation rights arranged with KADOKAWA CORPORATION, Tokyo, through TUTTLE-MORI AGENCY, INC., Tokyo.

Yen On
150 West 30th Street, 19th Floor
New York, NY 10001

Visit us at yenpress.com • facebook.com/yenpress • twitter.com/yenpress
yenpress.tumblr.com • instagram.com/yenpress

First Yen On Edition: July 2022
Edited by Yen On Editorial: Ivan Liang
Designed by Yen Press Design: Liz Parlett

Yen On is an imprint of Yen Press, LLC.
The Yen On name and logo are trademarks of Yen Press, LLC.

The publisher is not responsible for websites (or their content) that are not owned by the publisher.

Library of Congress Cataloging-in-Publication Data
Names: Yuumikan, author. I Koin, illustrator. I Cunningham, Andrew, 1979– translator.
Title: Bofuri, I don't want to get hurt, so I'll max out my defense / Yuumikan ; illustration by Koin ; translated by Andrew Cunningham.
Other titles: Itai no wa iya nano de bōgyoryoku ni kyokufuri shitai to omoimasu. English
Description: First Yen On edition. I New York : Yen On, 2021–
Identifiers: LCCN 2020055872 I ISBN 9781975322731 (v. 1 ; trade paperback) I
    ISBN 9781975323547 (v. 2 ; trade paperback) I ISBN 9781975323561 (v. 3 ; trade paperback) I
    ISBN 9781975323585 (v. 4 ; trade paperback) I ISBN 9781975323608 (v. 5 ; trade paperback) I
    ISBN 9781975323622 (v. 6 ; trade paperback)
Subjects: LCSH: Video gamers—Fiction. I Virtual reality—Fiction. I GSAFD: Science fiction.
Classification: LCC PL874.I46 I8313 2021 I DDC 895.63/6—dc23
LC record available at https://lccn.loc.gov/2020055872

ISBNs: 978-1-9753-2362-2 (paperback)
       978-1-9753-2363-9 (ebook)

10 9 8 7 6 5 4 3 2 1

LSC-C

Printed in the United States of America

CONTENTS

I Don't Want to Get Hurt,
so I'll Max Out My Defense.

NewWorld Online Status

|| NAME **Maple** || Maple LV **48**

HP 200/200 MP 22/22

STATUS

[STR] 000 [VIT] 11970 [AGI] 000 [DEX] 000 [INT] 000

EQUIPMENT

|| New Moon: Hydra || Night's Facsimile: Devour || Bonding Bridge

|| Black Rose Armor: Saturating Chaos || Toughness Ring || Life Ring

SKILLS

Shield Attack Sidestep Deflect Meditation Taunt Inspire HP Boost (S) MP Boost (S)

Green's Grace Great Shield Mastery VI Cover Move IV Cover Pierce Guard Counter

Quick Change Absolute Defense Moral Turpitude Giant Killing Hydra Eater Bomb Eater

Sheep Eater Indomitable Guardian Psychokinesis Fortress Martyr's Devotion Machine God

Bug Urn Curse Zone Freeze Pandemonium I

NewWorld Online Status

|| NAME **Sally** || Sally LV **44**

HP 32/32 MP 130/130

STATUS

[STR] 100 [VIT] 000 [AGI] 163 [DEX] 045 [INT] 050

EQUIPMENT

|| Deep Sea Dagger || Seabed Dagger

|| Surface Scarf: Mirage || Oceanic Coat: Oceanic

|| Oceanic Clothes || Black Boots || Bonding Bridge

SKILLS

Gale Slash Defense Break Inspire Down Attack Power Attack Switch Attack

Combo Blade V Martial Arts V Fire Magic III Water Magic III Wind Magic III Earth Magic II

Dark Magic II Light Magic II Strength Boost (S) Combo Boost (S) MP Boost (M) MP Cost Down (S)

MP Recovery Speed Boost (S) Poison Resist (S) Gathering Speed Boost (S) Dagger Mastery VIII

Magic Mastery III Affliction VI Presence Block II Presence Detect II Sneaky Steps I Leap III

Quick Change Cooking I Fishing Swimming X Diving X Shearing Superspeed

Ancient Ocean Chaser Blade Jack of All Trades Sword Dance Shed Skin Web Spinner VI

Ice Pillar Subzero Domain

Welcome to NewWorld Online

NAME **Chrome** HP 940/940 MP 52/52 LV 66

STATUS
STR 130 VIT 180 AGI 020 DEX 030 INT 010

EQUIPMENT
- Headhunter: Life Eater
- Wrath Wraith Wall: Soul Syphon
- Bloodstained Skull: Soul Eater
- Bloodstained Bone Armor: Dead or Alive
- Robust Ring
- Impregnable Ring
- Defense Ring

SKILLS
Thrust — Elemental Blade — Shield Attack — Sidestep — Deflect — Great Defense — Taunt — Impregnable Stance — Bulwark — HP Boost (L) — HP Recovery Speed Boost (L) — MP Boost (S) — Green's Grace — Great Shield Mastery X — Defense Mastery X — Cover Move X — Cover — Pierce Guard — Counter — Guard Aura — Defensive Formation — Guardian Power — Great Shield Secrets IV — Defense Secrets III — Paralyze Nullification — Poison Nullification — Stun Resist (L) — Sleep Resist (L) — Freeze Nullification — Burn Resist (L) — Mining IV — Gathering V — Shearing — Spirit Light — Indomitable Guardian — Battle Healing — Reaper's Mire

NAME **Iz** HP 100/100 MP 100/100 LV 52

STATUS
STR 045 VIT 020 AGI 080 DEX 210 INT 050

EQUIPMENT
- Blacksmith Hammer X
- Alchemist Goggles: Faustian Alchemy
- Alchemist Long Coat: Magic Workshop
- Blacksmith Leggings X
- Alchemist Boots: New Frontier
- Potion Pouch
- Item Pouch
- Black Gloves

SKILLS
Strike — Crafting Mastery X — Crafting Secrets IV — Enhance Success Rate Boost (L) — Gathering Speed Boost (L) — Mining Speed Boost (L) — Affliction II — Sneaky Steps III — Smithing X — Sewing X — Horticulture X — Synthesizing X — Augmentation X — Cooking X — Mining X — Gathering X — Swimming IV — Diving V — Shearing — Godsmith's Grace X

NAME **Kanade** HP 335/335 MP 290/290 LV 38

STATUS
STR 015 VIT 010 AGI 045 DEX 050 INT 110

EQUIPMENT
- Divine Wisdom: Akashic Records
- Diamond Newsboy Cap VIII
- Smart Coat VI
- Smart Leggings VIII
- Smart Boots VI
- Spade Earrings
- Mage Gloves
- Holy Ring

SKILLS
Magic Mastery VI — MP Boost (M) — MP Cost Down (S) — MP Recovery Speed Boost (L) — Magic Boost (S) — Green's Grace — Fire Magic IV — Water Magic III — Wind Magic IV — Earth Magic II — Dark Magic II — Light Magic V — Sorcerer's Stacks — Reaper's Mire

NAME **Kasumi** HP 435/435 MP 70/70 LV 62

STATUS
STR 185 VIT 080 AGI 090 DEX 030 INT 020

EQUIPMENT
Yukari, the All-Consuming Blight		Cherry Blossom Barrette
Cherry Blossom Vestments		Edo Purple Hakama		Samurai Greaves
Samurai Gauntlets		Gold Obi Fastener		Cherry Blossom Crest

SKILLS
Gleam Helmsplitter Guard Break Sweep Slice Eye for Attack Inspire Attack Stance Katana Arts X Cleave Throw HP Boost (L) MP Boost (M) Poison Nullification Paralyze Nullification Stun Resist (L) Sleep Resist (M) Freeze Resist (M) Burn Resist (S) Longsword Mastery X Katana Mastery X Longsword Secrets II Katana Secrets II Mining IV Gathering VI Diving V Swimming VI Leap VII Shearing Keen Sight Indomitable Sword Spirit Dauntless Sinew Superspeed Ever Vigilant

---

NAME **Mai** HP 35/35 MP 20/20 LV 36

STATUS
STR 360 VIT 000 AGI 000 DEX 000 INT 000

EQUIPMENT
| Black Annihilammer VIII | | Black Doll Dress VIII | | Black Doll Tights VIII |
| Black Doll Shoes VIII | | Little Ribbon | | Silk Gloves |

SKILLS
Double Stamp Double Impact Double Strike Attack Boost (M) Hammer Mastery VI Throw Farshot Conqueror Annihilator Giant Killing

---

NAME **Yui** HP 35/35 MP 20/20 LV 36

STATUS
STR 360 VIT 000 AGI 000 DEX 000 INT 000

EQUIPMENT
| White Annihilammer VIII | | White Doll Dress VIII | | White Doll Tights VIII |
| White Doll Shoes VIII | | Little Ribbon | | Silk Gloves |

SKILLS
Double Stamp Double Impact Double Strike Attack Boost (M) Hammer Mastery VI Throw Farshot Conqueror Annihilator Giant Killing

Defense Build and Items

During the sixth event, Maple had spent some time in a jungle where HP recovery was impossible. She'd met up with Pain, the guild master of the Order of the Holy Sword and one of the best players in the game. Her defensive skills kept him safe, and together they conquered the jungle. Maple spent much of this outing in Atrocity form with Pain on her back, and he looked rather aghast the whole time—but that was *his* problem.

While she thoroughly enjoyed herself, Maple had no luck getting the items required to make a jungle run, and her attention soon shifted to stories Chrome had told her about the stratum map.

In the course of investigating his findings, she stumbled upon a boss called the King of Light—who promptly sent her packing. Of course, Maple wasn't one to give up that easily. She bought a ton of items in preparation to head out and try again.

A few days after her shopping trip, Maple was walking beneath the thunderheads again.

"Can I win this time? I'm not so sure."

She was feeling a trifle nervous, but her inventory was stuffed full of purchases she'd acquired just for this battle.

If any of them proved effective, it could be the key that would decide the entire fight.

"Or they could be completely useless. Welp, if I try everything and none of it works, I'll just have to come up with a new plan!"

Once more, the throne loomed before her.

"Okay! Let's do this!"

As she stepped into range, light appeared above, coalescing into a seated humanoid form.

A divine glow appeared at ground level, and arrows of light began shooting.

"Those don't bother me!"

This time, Maple wasn't fighting back. She let the arrows hit her as she simply walked right up to the base of the throne.

Once she reached the King of Light's feet, she opened her inventory, checking the contents even as more missiles rained down upon her.

"Hmm…let's go one at a time."

Maple pulled a piece of paper out of her inventory and stuck it to the king's feet.

After a burst of red light and a roar, the paper went up in flames.

"Aw, it didn't work! Guess that rules out fire. Next!"

She plastered another piece of paper onto her foe.

Crack. The feet froze.

"Oh, the HP went down a bit! Nice."

Her inventory still open, Maple sat down by the king's feet and busied herself pasting paper after paper to them.

By diligently freezing the king's toes, she managed to carve off 10 percent of its health.

*   *   *

"Hmm…I'm all out. Guess it's time to try something else."

Maple switched to a new item, and when that ran out, she switched to another. Slowly but surely, she was grinding away at the boss's health.

As she did, the boss's attacks grew more intense and started applying status effects, but they all just bounced off Maple, so she paid them no heed.

"Hmm, I've used all the magic attack items. Fire and wind did nothing, so I guess I'll stow them away. Maybe they'll be useful someday. Hrmm…"

Maple eyed the king's health bar.

She'd certainly made a dent, but it had only dropped to 60 percent at best.

The items she'd used just hadn't done that much damage, so this was no surprise.

It seemed like the only way to do any real damage to the King of Light was to use really expensive, super-effective items.

"Guess we'll see what this does next!"

Maple pulled out a red rock just small enough to fit in the palm of her hand.

She flung it at the king's feet, and it exploded, doing damage.

"Sweet!"

Maple had arrived at this strategy after overhearing some chatter in town.

This item was quite cheap, and it randomly dealt a fixed amount of damage one to three times to any target.

The reason she'd been listening in was that the players had been wondering if using the item might be an effective tactic against *her*.

They'd eventually concluded that it would be far simpler to use piercing skills, but Maple didn't know that.

"Don't worry. There's more where that came from!" Maple kept throwing rocks, and the King of Light's HP was steadily declining.

It certainly was taking a while, but since Maple was the only one doing any damage, her life wasn't in any danger.

The outcome would hinge on the huge quantity of red stones she had stuffed into her inventory.

"Finally! *Finally!* Halfway! Mm?"

Just as Maple's stoning got her to the midpoint of the boss's HP bar, two angels appeared, one on either side of it.

They fluttered into the air and began shooting arrows at Maple.

"As if that's gonna work—uh, hold on. What the...?"

The arrows were wrapping Maple in golden thread, tying her to the clouds beneath her feet.

When she tried to move, the threads stretched—and did *not* break.

"Huh...and I'm losing MP. Whatever! Not my problem!"

This was clearly an ensnaring attack, so it would have reduced her AGI, but no matter how big the penalty, there was no way to have less than zero. Maple was more or less totally unaffected.

"Back to work!"

Maple turned back toward the King of Light, stone in hand—

And spotted a *halo* over its head. And furthermore—giant wings, made of light, passing right through the back of the throne.

But worst of all (from Maple's point of view) was that his HP was slowly recovering.

"Huh?! No, stop that!"

Maple quickly started hurling rocks again, but it was recovering health faster than she could hurt it. She'd used so many items getting the boss's health this low, and it had just healed right back up.

"Not fair! Is this legal?!"

Maple drew her sword and poked the king's feet with it, but this did no damage.

"Urgh…that blows. Well, I bought these by accident, but let's try them anyway!"

She flipped through her inventory some more and dropped a bunch of fermentation weights on its toes.

These were sold by the same shop as the red stones, and she'd been so preoccupied with buying those up that she'd accidentally grabbed a bunch of rocks meant for making pickles.

Rather than resell them, she'd hung on to them in the faint hope that they might one day prove useful. This was not that day.

"I'm so done…*sigh*…"

Still caught in innumerable golden threads while arrows continued raining down around her, Maple trudged away.

"Ugh, what a waste of money…"

She logged out and spent the rest of the day in bed, looking uncharacteristically cross.

The next day Maple was back—with Mai and Yui in tow.

"Wow, that's a *lot* of lightning."

"Eek…that one startled me."

"You get used to it!" Maple said, smiling. Glittering wings adorned her back.

"Um, so today…"

"Yeah, it won't take long. Thanks for helping!"

Maple bowed her head.

"No, the jungle's way too big for us, and we keep tripping over stuff, so...we kinda gave up on it. Right?"

"Yep... Like Yui says, we were actually looking for something else to do!"

The twins insisted this would go toward paying Maple back for the time she'd helped them with a quest on the fourth stratum, so the trio traveled to the throne together, ready for attempt number three.

"You're going down this time for sure!" Maple declared, glaring up at the King of Light.

The outcome was all too obvious.

Maple surged forward, the twins kept safe in the embrace of her angel form.

The arrows of light proved no detriment, and they closed in, slowly but surely.

When they reached the king's feet, Maple waved the twins forward.

"Just a second!"

They used a number of items Iz had given them.

These granted them a red aura—a visible sign of their boosted attack.

Then each took out two hammers, and they were ready to go.

"Oh, right! Inspire!"

This was a skill Maple had obtained in the second event but almost never used.

It provided a temporary 20 percent boost to Mai and Yui's STR.

And a 20 percent boost to their STR would give them far more DPS than Maple's red-stone tactic could dish out.

Perhaps this last buff was unnecessary, but the twins stepped up, ready to flatten the king—literally.

""Double Strike!""

With a sound like thunder, each hammer hit twice, and since there were two sets of them, eight crashes rang out. The boss's HP was instantly reduced to nothing, and only silence remained.

The king's light scattered, glittering as it faded away.

Some of it fell around them, accompanied by a voice informing them of their new skill.

"Woo! Ha-ha! You summoned two angels last time, so I just did the same thing. Can't complain about that! Anywho, let's check out this skill."

Maple opened her menu.

Heaven's Throne

While seated on the throne, reduce incoming damage by 20% and heal for 2% HP per second. Effect lasts until the skill is deactivated or the skill user is incapacitated. While active, anyone within thirty yards (including the skill user) will be unable to use any skills with Attribute: Evil. Five-minute cooldown.

"Oh, maybe that's why."

In her first battle, several of Maple's skills had been sealed, giving her a real headache.

Quite a few of Maple's better skills were on the evil side.

"Let's try it out! Heaven's Throne!"

Light appeared right behind Maple, forming a throne just like the King of Light's—only Maple's size.

She gingerly took a seat, and as she settled down, white light poured out of the ground around her.

It was faint, but there was also a glow surrounding Maple herself.

Like the king's before her, Maple's wings went right through the back of the throne, glimmering behind it.

"Wow...nice! And pretty."

For the simple reason that she liked the way it looked, this instantly went to the top of the list of skills Maple planned to pro-actively use.

This might put a dent in her offensive potential, but it wasn't like Maple had been actively seeking out evil skills in the first place.

Maple was sitting on her throne, swinging her legs.

"Um, Maple?" Yui asked. "What is *that*?"

"Mm? Wait, didn't you get this skill, too?"

"No, we got a skill that lets us summon those arrows of light. But its effectiveness doesn't scale with STR, so I don't think we'll get much use out of it."

Maple had to think about that one.

Why had they gotten different skills?

The most obvious explanation was Martyr's Devotion—the angelic skill she still had active.

"The king had wings, too. Maybe that's it?! The description didn't mention anything."

Maple got off her throne, ready to take the twins home.

As she stood up, the glow radiating from her and the ground vanished.

"Oh, right! I have to be sitting. Oh, well! Should we head back?"

""Yep!""

"Hmm? Hang on."

She took one step, then turned back. Maple stroked her jaw, the wheels in her mind turning.

Sometime later…

A turtle was flying through the lightning, a throne on its back, and a glowing circle on the ground below.

"Syrup, are you sure it's not too heavy?"

Maple was sitting atop the throne currently situated on her pet's back.

This arrangement didn't seem to bother Syrup in the slightest.

"I think I'm gonna ride Syrup like this from now on. Plus, I can still use Machine God… Yeah, I like it!"

"Maple, we're almost out of the lightning field," Yui said, pointing at the expanse of white clouds ahead.

"Looks like it! I'm open to suggestions."

"Um…could we grind some levels?" Mai suggested.

The twins were still underleveled for this stratum.

"It's been hard surviving fights against anything we can't one-shot."

"Hmm. I guess I could use some levels, too. Haven't done much grinding lately."

Even as they spoke, the dazzling circle of light moved along the ground beneath them.

Syrup had carried the throne into the regular part of the map.

And naturally, there were *witnesses* to this spectacle.

One greatsworder was staring up at it in awe.

"There she goes…and…"

He frowned at the ground below.

"...why is it *glowing?*"

----

286 Name: Anonymous Spear Master
Maple's been quiet lately.

287 Name: Anonymous Archer
Other than making the ground freeze.

288 Name: Anonymous Mage
Lots of people can do that.
Why not Maple?

289 Name: Anonymous Greatsworder
She was flying around with a giant white throne on her turtle's back.
Made the ground light up like a disco ball.

290 Name: Anonymous Spear Master
Me and my big mouth.

291 Name: Anonymous Mage
I know people keep saying she's the Demon Lord, but now she's literally got the throne to go with it.

292 Name: Anonymous Archer
Definitely sounds holy, though.
Goes with the whole angel thing.

293 Name: Anonymous Great Shielder
Wut. This is news to me.

*   *   *

294 Name: Anonymous Greatsworder
Uh, I think she just used a skill while riding the turtle and it gave her a throne, but what it *does*, I dunno.
So I tried going under her, but there was no divine retribution for getting too close or anything.
I was half-expecting to die.

295 Name: Anonymous Spear Master
Shellback thrones are not normal.
Those usually go on the floor.

296 Name: Anonymous Great Shielder
Chances are it's something recovery or defense focused... Don't sound like a big AOE finisher, at least.

297 Name: Anonymous Mage
I don't want her firing anything that scary sitting down.
Please stahp, Maple.

298 Name: Anonymous Archer
If it's a throne skill, sitting is probably mandatory.
Then again, this is Maple we're talking about. It's not crazy to think she could work around that somehow.

299 Name: Anonymous Great Shielder
Not like she's highly mobile to begin with.
Meaning it's mostly upside for her.

300 Name: Anonymous Greatsworder
Apparently, she can summon two giant ogres to boot.

Like, several yards tall.
Badass!

301 Name: Anonymous Spear Master
Her army of minions grows larger...
She's definitely the Demon Lord. Tell her to paint the throne black.

302 Name: Anonymous Archer
Sounds OP.
Someone tell me what Maple's confirmed powers are again?

303 Name: Anonymous Mage
Poison. Instadeath shield. Monster summons. Monster transformation. Angel form.
Artillery. Ground freezing (new!). Ogre summons (new!). Thrones (new!).
And still hella tanky.

304 Name: Anonymous Great Shielder
We sure she didn't spawn inside a dungeon?

305 Name: Anonymous Greatsworder
I hope the real last boss is weaker.

306 Name: Anonymous Mage
It better be, or no one'll beat it.
Guess we'll find out about the throne in the next PVP event.

307 Name: Anonymous Spear Master
Gotta bank on Pain's heroism.

*   *   *

308 Name: Anonymous Archer
I got mowed down like a rando villager.
I was guarding an orb and something slunk out of the dark... Still can't believe it was Maple.

309 Name: Anonymous Great Shielder
She's still human, deep down.

310 Name: Anonymous Spear Master
If that ever changes, she really will become a boss.

311 Name: Anonymous Greatsworder
A raid boss?
Nice to see her still going strong, though.

312 Name: Anonymous Archer
Yeah...
She might be getting stronger even as we speak.

313 Name: Anonymous Mage
Scary yet cute.

CHAPTER 1

Defense Build and Umbrellas

The event came to a close while Maple was still flying around on Heaven's Throne.

She never did make it back to the jungle.

As things wound down and everyone was ready for a breather from grinding, Maple found herself back at the Guild Home.

"I didn't even realize the event ended! It was just way too hard to get those jungle tickets."

As Maple thought about what to do next, Sally came in the door.

She waved Sally over.

"Sup, Maple. Any luck in the jungle? I came out decently."

From the grin on her face, she must be pretty happy with her haul.

"Mm…not really. I gave up and just explored the normal map instead."

"Ah…no luck with tickets? Well, find anything interesting on this side?"

"Totally!" Maple said, her face lighting up.

"Yeah? What?"

"A throne!"

"Um. Sorry, come again?"

"……? I got a throne!"

"Riiight…"

That alone seemed to give Sally a sense of the implications, and she settled onto the couch next to Maple.

Sally had been hitting the jungles hard, so they hadn't seen each other in a while. Between Maple's new throne and Sally's jungle adventures, there was no lack of things they needed to catch up on.

And eventually the conversation turned to the next stratum.

"With the event over, it might not be long till they add a new level."

"Oh yeah. Wonder what it'll be like? I hope it's pretty."

Maple's mind was on fantastic sights to come.

Beautiful ocean vistas, murmuring forests, bustling towns…

"So if you've got anything left to do here, better get it done."

"That makes it sound like you've got a place in mind, Sally."

"Kinda. You hit the place with the slow rain yet? Wanna try and clear it?"

This was an area Chrome and Kasumi had found.

The fifth stratum's motif was an illusory world nestled among the clouds, and it had none of your typical forests and fields. The ground was all fluffy white and so were the dungeon walls. While the map reflected this, dangerous areas were marked with lightning—or slow-falling rain.

Sally explained that someone else had already cleared this area and the reward was now public knowledge.

"Oh, but Sally, you haven't been to the lightning zone yet, right?"

"No need. The skills you mentioned don't sound like my thing."

"Roger. In that case…shall we?"

"Yep. Let's get ready and hit up the slow rain."

Preparations did not take long.

As they reached the building exit, it opened from the outside.

"Oh, Maple, Sally. Where you headed?"

It was Kasumi, swinging by the Guild Home because she didn't have anything better to do.

"We're headed to the slow-rain area. Thanks for the tip-off!"

"Oh, *that* place… Actually, mind if join you?" Kasumi asked. This sounded like the perfect opportunity.

Naturally, Maple and Sally had no reason to refuse. The three of them set out together.

"So, uh, Kasumi, you pick one up yet?"

"No, afraid not. I was busy with the event."

"……?"

Maple had no clue what they were talking about.

Seeing that, Sally threw a riddle at her.

"Maple, what do you need when it's raining outside?"

"Er, I guess…an umbrella?"

A shot in the dark.

"Exactly! You gotta have one to get through the slow rain."

"So our first order of business is to go umbrella shopping. We know where they're sold."

Kasumi and Sally led the way, Maple in tow.

After a quick stroll, they reached the umbrella shop.

It was a tiny store filled with rows of umbrellas in all shapes, sizes, and hues.

"Hmm, which one…?"

"They all do the same thing."

"Yeah, I get that," Maple said, but she kept prowling the shop, searching for the right umbrella.

"I'm going with this one."

"Simple is best."

Kasumi chose a dark red while Sally opted for a blue that matched her outfit.

"Maple is...over there. Uh, what *is* that?"

Maple was holding an umbrella made entirely of fluffy clouds.

"It's a limited item!"

"That phrase is like your only weakness."

"Hrk...I know, but...it works like a normal umbrella, see?"

She opened up her first choice and twirled it overhead.

"I assume if they're selling it as a regular product, it's functional, so...it shouldn't be a problem, right? Probably?"

Kasumi found it hard to make definitive statements when Maple was involved.

All three of them made their purchases in short order, and they continued on toward the slow-rain zone.

◆□◆□◆□◆□◆

They ran into several monsters on the way, but that didn't even slow down this party.

They bulldozed their way right to their destination.

"Looks like it's still coming down. Maple, umbrella time."

"Gotcha!"

Maple fished the cloudbrella out of her inventory. Sally and Kasumi followed suit.

"The umbrellas protect you from anything falling, but if a drop lands nearby, try to dodge the spray."

"Will do! Let's go!"

Umbrellas held high, they ventured into the slow rain.

"See? It's not getting through!"

Maple could feel drops striking the umbrella above her and was relieved to find it really wasn't porous.

Her umbrella didn't exactly *look* like an umbrella, but it worked just fine.

"That shop wasn't kidding about their merchandise, then," Sally said. "We've got a bit of a hike ahead of us, so let me brief you on your role in the boss fight, Maple."

She quickly laid out the basic strategy.

"Mm-hmm, I can do that!" Maple said, nodding. It was fairly straightforward.

"Heads up," Kasumi said. "We're here."

She folded her umbrella.

The skies above were still cloudy, but there was no more rainfall.

Maple and Sally put their umbrellas away, getting ready for action.

After completing last-minute preparations, all three stepped into the boss's domain.

"Here it comes!"

Before them, a mass of water seeped through the clouds, rising from the ground in a humanoid form.

The surface of it rippled, and within that water floated a blue lump.

That blue bit was the boss's core—its weak point.

And as its shape coalesced, the clouds above began to change.

"More rain incoming, Maple!"

"Yep, just like you said!"

"That's all yours, girls."

Each of them knew her job and sprang into action.

And in response, the boss's liquid body shifted, its arms becoming swords.

It moved toward them, feet squelching on the clouds below.

Meanwhile, the skies opened, releasing not rain*drops* but orbs of water over a yard across.

At the same time that Kasumi charged the boss, Sally activated two skills in rapid succession.

"First up, Oceanic! Then Subzero Domain!"

The first created a puddle, and the second froze it, coating the ground in a layer of frost.

"Perfect. Web Spinner! Ice Pillar!"

Sally used two more skills, and Maple watched in awe as she used her webs to scurry up the side of the pillar.

"Wow! That's so cool! Oops, time for me to get going, too. Full Deploy!"

Maple aimed her weapons at the sky.

She had two jobs.

The first was to break the water orbs as Sally froze them. Since this would likely make the boss target Maple, her second job was to soak its attacks.

Maple began firing into the air, shattering the chunks of ice as fast as Sally could freeze them.

This tactic was effective because they didn't let the orbs come near them even after freezing all the water in midair.

Like the surrounding slow rain, these watery orbs would apply a speed debuff if they hit any of the players.

Their strategy hinged on not letting that happen.

*　　*　　*

"Wow, Sally's bounding all over the place…," Maple murmured in awe.

She was watching Sally jump from pillar to pillar, freezing all the rain orbs overhead.

"That's so cool!"

Maple's eyes were gleaming in pure admiration, but pulling this amazing feat off required untold amounts of effort, even for Sally.

"Right Hand: Web, Right Hand: Contract, Left Hand: Web, Left Foot: Web, Left Hand: Contract, Right Foot: Web, Right Hand: Web, Right Hand: Contract, Left Hand: Web!"

To control her webs, she had to constantly rattle out commands.

It was an excruciatingly careful ballet of creating webs, contracting them, and canceling them with impeccable timing.

She soared through the skies, constantly monitoring her webs all the while.

Coming to a stop on an ice pillar, she took a moment to catch her breath.

"Whew, that's one stage down. If we let these orbs fall, we'd all be snails… The next part isn't any easier, so I can't let up now."

Once they'd shattered a number of orbs, the boss changed tactics.

It had been busy pummeling Maple's head with its swords, but now its core shifted, slipping into the clouds underfoot.

They didn't have to wait long before several cores emerged, making copies of the boss.

The more rainwater fell, the more copies would appear, and the

harder it would become to find the real core. Since Maple's party had handled the orbs well, the boss only made the minimum number of copies.

"Looks like our plan worked. It's time for Blood Blade!"

Now it was Kasumi's turn. The cursed sword in her hand transformed into a dark red liquid.

This temporarily halved Kasumi's HP—

But the results were absolutely worth it. Her Blood Blade shot out in all directions, hurtling through the air and running along the ground, staining the clouds red as she hit every core at once.

"When in doubt, just stab everything!"

Once the attack ended, Kasumi's blade went back to normal, returning to her hand.

In a solo fight, this was a risky skill, but with Maple keeping the boss busy, she could safely take full advantage.

"I think doing that three more times should be enough. This boss definitely makes you work for it."

"Kasumi! Potion!"

"Thanks!"

If they let even a single orb fall, she wouldn't be able to hit every core, and the tide of the battle would slowly but surely turn against them. Until the boss went down, there would be no margin for error.

The second stage of the final boss fight on this stratum had begun. It would only get harder from here on out.

That said, what they actually *did* wasn't much different.

Kasumi and Sally both knew exactly how the boss's attack patterns changed in each phase. (Maple not so much.)

Making it through the first phase made them confident they could pull this off.

"The rain's falling faster! Sally's...got it covered."

Each stage of the boss fight they cleared meant more orbs that moved faster and faster.

Since Maple was keeping the boss itself thoroughly preoccupied, Kasumi could afford to keep her head on a swivel, ready to step in if Sally couldn't freeze an orb in time.

But Sally was flawlessly taking them out, so she was mostly just admiring Sally's performance.

"Sally's conquered the sky, too. I guess she's still relatively normal compared to Maple...I think?"

Technically speaking, Sally was merely jumping from pillar to pillar and not literally flying. *Technically.*

"I bet she could go absolutely nuts in a forest. With less slippery footholds, her mobility would be even more dizzying to look at."

But while Kasumi pictured that, the boss's core moved again, creating slightly more copies than before.

"Blood Blade!"

At the cost of yet more HP, her red blade spread out, once again destroying every core.

"I can hit that number, too? Hmm. Definitely more versatile than Purple Phantom Blade. Of course, the damage isn't as high..."

Kasumi's persistent core hunting was apparently enough to draw the boss's aggro.

However, this monster was on the slow side, and her AGI proved more than enough to keep her out of its reach. This boss had only gotten the opportunity to pummel Maple because she was so *slow*—and, more to the point, hadn't bothered evading at all.

"It should start using ranged attacks alongside the rain right about now..."

And since Kasumi was well aware of what each new stage would bring, she was not about to be caught flat-footed.

*　　*　　*

Ultimately, Sally never let a single orb hit the ground, and the boss remained at a disadvantage.

Maple never ran out of ammo, and Kasumi didn't get hit even once.

Their plan went off without a hitch.

When the last Blood Blade pierced the final core, the boss crumbled away.

"Aww, I didn't get a chance to bust out my secret weapon."

Maple was disappointed she hadn't gotten to use her throne. Sally came sliding down the ice pillar and trotted over.

"Whew…first time slinging these in a real fight, but it sure is exhausting. I don't think the devs meant for the skill to be used this way."

She started doing stretches.

"You were amazing, Sally!"

"Mm? Was I? Sweet. I can't exactly fly alongside you, Maple, but maybe someday we can team up for some aerial combat."

"Hey, you two! It dropped some items!" Kasumi called.

They ran over and checked out their loot.

Rain Crystal

Creates up to three water orbs that inflict a 50% AGI debuff on contact. One-minute cooldown.

Sally didn't waste any time trying it out, and the orbs it made were a good twenty inches across. They slowly wobbled away.

"Looks like the orbs vanish if they take damage. I dunno… maybe you could use them as footholds, Sally?"

"That was my thought. Worth a try anyway. Seems pretty hard to hit anyone with these…"

If Sally combined the orbs with her Ice Pillar, she might be able to gain even more air time. That was one reason she'd wanted to come here.

"Is there any way for me to use them?" Maple wondered. "I suppose I could try it if anyone pops out right in front of me."

They would certainly be quite effective at such close range, but whether Maple would have the wherewithal to remember that option was a separate matter.

But this was the last thing they'd had to do on this floor; they'd be spending the rest of their time here waiting for the next event or stratum.

"Time to hit the road?"

"You know it."

But before they could turn to go, they saw an impish grin on Maple's face.

"Heaven's Throne!" she yelled.

A white throne appeared behind her.

"Um……?!"

"Wha—?!"

They gaped at Maple, then hastily looked around.

"Ha! I just wanted to show it off. Well? Surprised? Pretty, ain't it?"

Maple was all smiles.

"Sure…but it wasn't the aesthetics that startled us."

"Then again, this is pretty much par for the course with Maple."

"……?"

Maple had no idea what Kasumi meant by that.

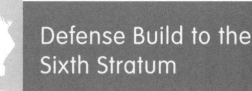

CHAPTER 2

Defense Build to the Sixth Stratum

Time passed, as it is wont to do. Before long, early March arrived.

A dungeon on the fifth floor now contained a path to the next stratum.

A few early birds had already run it, and now it was Maple Tree's turn to do the same.

"The boss this time is a jellyfish made of clouds," Kasumi explained. "It uses a slew of different status effects."

Chrome and Sally frowned.

"Do physical attacks work at all?" Chrome asked.

"Yes."

"In that case…we've got Mai and Yui," Sally pointed out.

Chrome's eyes narrowed. "Does it have *piercing* damage?"

"No one mentioned it," Kasumi said.

Chrome visibly relaxed. "Then we're set."

"Yup."

"That's right."

All Maple Tree members were present and accounted for.

They could tackle the boss in peak form.

These three spoke of victory not from arrogance but as a matter of course.

While plans were being laid, Iz and the others were getting ready in the back. They soon emerged into the main living room.

"Let's go! Get this over with and hit the sixth stratum!"

"Should we take Syrup for a ride?" Maple suggested.

Everyone agreed, and the entire guild climbed aboard, bobbing on turtleback across the sea of clouds.

◆□◆□◆□◆□◆

"And we're here!"

Syrup settled onto the ground as they came in for a landing. Maple gave it a nice head rub before returning it to her ring.

"We ready?"

"Maple in front! Kasumi and I'll take the rear. Just in case," Chrome said.

This really was nothing but a precaution. Even as he spoke, Maple was activating Martyr's Devotion.

"Well, sometimes things cancel your skills…," he said.

With the twins in the center, the party headed down the narrow passage.

Mai and Yui were generally kept heavily guarded until the boss fight, where their true potential could be unleashed.

"I mean, I think Maple could win this on her own."

"I entirely agree."

Kasumi and Chrome nodded at each other just as Maple's shield gobbled up a thundercloud.

"Onward! March!"

The road was too narrow for ambushes, and as long as she had uses of Devour left, she could vanquish all challengers just by holding her shield in front of her.

If she'd been running this solo, she'd have filled these corridors with poison, so this was Maple being considerate.

Any monsters capable of slowing Maple down were overqualified to be trash mobs and would never be on this map in the first place.

On her own, Maple's odds of making a wrong turn (or accidentally going to the wrong dungeon entirely) were fairly high, but this time she had Sally navigating for her, and they made it to the boss room in style.

They opened the doors and stepped in. The room itself was made out of clouds—and as they entered, the downy ceiling began to *move*.

Wispy tentacles also made of clouds extended downward, and the jellyfish followed.

"Wow! That looks so fluffy!"

"It's poisonous, though. Maple, you keep it busy."

"Roger!"

Maple began horsing around with the jellyfish.

The tentacles had a paralytic effect, but it didn't affect her. If anything, she found it rather pleasant.

The boss was hitting her pretty hard, but the impact seemed only to knock the tentacles back.

Behind her, Mai and Yui were standing just at the edge of Maple's protection, loaded up with buffs and waiting for their moment.

They didn't have to wait long.

"Here we go!"

"Looking good…!"

Certain Maple had its full attention, the twins stepped forward, each carrying two hammers bigger than herself.

Spotting their approach, Maple said, "Okay, Mr. Jellyfish. I *am* sorry, but we need to beat you."

She gave the fluffy tentacles one last forlorn pat and stepped aside.

""Double Stamp!""

"Keep going, Mai!"

"On it, Yui!"

The jellyfish took a pounding before being flung aside and crumbling into mist before it could even turn its tentacles toward the new threats.

"Should've had more physical resistance if it wanted to survive that," Kanade said.

"I thought the same thing," Iz agreed.

These two had been responsible for the bulk of the buffs on the twins.

But as they pointed out, the cause of this travesty also lay with the boss design.

Thus the party of eight cleared the fight without breaking a sweat and headed for the sixth stratum.

"I wonder what it's like, Sally."

"Hmm, I didn't actually check. Heh, I thought it would be more fun if we found out together."

"Eh-heh-heh, that *does* sound fun."

"I'm cool with whatever, but…if my webs turn out to be useful, that'd be ideal."

The entrance to the sixth stratum loomed overhead.

*　　*　　*

Maple Tree stepped through, finding itself in a wasteland—and the remains of an ancient cemetery.

A thin mist shrouded the area, making even the moon above seem sinister.

"Whoa…what's this?"

Maple felt something clutch her hand and looked toward it.

"N-not cool…," Sally said, visibly pale.

Scary levels are a video game staple, and *NewWorld Online* had clearly gone with that theme for the sixth map.

As always, their first stop was the Guild Home.

Sally never once let go of Maple's hand. Her gaze darted nervously in every direction, and it wasn't because she was on the lookout for incoming enemies.

Their new Guild Home *looked* like an abandoned building, but inside, it was just as cozy as on previous stratums.

While everyone else hit up their rooms or scoped out the other amenities, Maple and Sally huddled up in the living room.

"*Sigh*… Okay, I'm good."

Sally brought up her menu, ready to sign off.

"Welp, Maple…guess I'll see you when they add the seventh stratum."

"Whaa?!"

Sally managed a listless smile and vanished before Maple could say another word.

She'd wanted to run away so bad she'd literally quit out of the game. Maple knew full well just how much Sally hated horror, so she took this in stride.

"Looks like I can't explore with her this time…"

Just as Maple didn't want to get hurt, Sally didn't want to be scared.

"Judging by what she said…Sally's really not coming back for a while."

Maple decided there was no use hoping for the impossible and set off to explore the town on her own.

Outside the Guild Home, she looked around, wondering where to go first.

"Mm! Let's just look at *everything*. That way when Sally comes back, I can tell her where everything is!"

All fired up, Maple began wandering the moonlit avenues.

"Man, everything's in ruins. I bet all these buildings look normal insi— Mm?"

A few buildings were completely collapsed, and as she passed them, winds brushed the back of her neck…some hot, some cold.

But when Maple turned around, there was nothing there.

"Yeah, it'd be impossible for Sally to handle this place at night."

She caught a glimpse of a blue wisp floating behind a window. Sally was always way more perceptive than Maple. There was little doubt she'd be all too aware of these happenings.

"Welp, let's try out a shop!"

Maple found a building with lights on and stepped inside.

While Maple was out exploring—

Risa was curled up in bed in the real world.

"Nope, nope, nope. Absolutely not going back. And I'm sure it's fine. I'll just catch up on the next stratum."

She sprawled out like she had come to terms with her decision, but it didn't take her long to start reading up on the sixth stratum.

And one of the first tidbits she found was about how to get an MP-increasing skill.

"Kanade could use that…so could I, really. A race? Against a skeleton?! NOPE."

One look at the enemy and Risa let out a moan.

She kept looking for the latest posts. Intel was still scarce, but people had already started finding new skills and items that had been placed in obvious locations.

She read about one skill that inflicted status effects and another that had a low chance of doubling an item's effect. There was also a skill that buffed AGI.

Worse, she found stories about a pair of shoes that made a single invisible platform in the air. The third stratum's flying machines didn't work on other maps, so she'd given up on being able to move like that anywhere else. Perhaps there was hope after all.

"Argh. Hngg…urghhh. Mmm! Auuuugh…!"

Making a serious of horrible noises, Risa ran her fingers down the screen. But the words refused to change.

Risa spent a while psyching herself up to sign in, abandoning the idea, and then trying once again—ultimately to no avail. In the end, she simply collapsed on her bed in weary defeat.

CHAPTER 3

Defense Build and the Haunted Mansion

Several days had passed since the sixth stratum's launch.

Maple was once again logged into *NWO*.

Today she was visiting the Guild Home for repairs on her archangel gear.

Maple didn't normally take damage, but her equipment sure did.

"…By the looks of these scratches, monster attacks are getting plenty powerful."

"I've gotta raise my defense even higher!"

"My dwindling potion supplies are speaking volumes."

Maple took her gear back from Iz and returned them to her Quick Change slots.

"Welp, off to explore!"

Just as Maple was about to leave, the front door opened—and the last person she'd expected came in.

"*Gasp!* Sally?!"

"Oh…Maple…"

"Whaaaat?! You came back?!"

Maple looked dumbfounded, so Sally awkwardly explained herself.

It seemed that there were simply too many things she couldn't let slip through her fingers.

Well aware that heading out of town on her own was a recipe for failure, Sally had come by the home hoping someone could help.

"Got it, got it. I'd be happy to help. I didn't really have anything particular in mind anyway."

"You...have no idea how much I appreciate this."

"Let's get a move on!"

It was rare to see Sally this cowed, but Maple took her hand and pulled her out of their home.

Maple took Sally out onto the field by the hand. Once they were outside, she summoned Syrup, Giganticized it, and climbed up onto its shell. She patted it gently as she said, "Thanks... Martyr's Devotion! Heaven's Throne!"

Once her throne appeared on Syrup's back, Maple took a seat. Sally settled on the shell in front of her, eyes tightly closed.

After they were in place, Maple asked Syrup to levitate and stand by.

"Sally, where to?"

"There's a mansion to the west of town...over that way."

"Got it. Westward ho!"

Syrup banked obediently, and their flight was soon underway.

"*Sigh...* This is where it gets baaaad..."

Sally was hunched up on the shell, face buried in her hands.

They gracefully wove through the air for a while.

"Ah!" Maple yelped.

"Huh? What...?" Sally made the mistake of looking up.

There was a pale-faced woman floating right in front of them. Her hands reached out and brushed Sally's face.

"..........!!"

"Full Deploy! Commence Assault!"

Sally threw herself on Maple just as the bullets disintegrated the ghost.

"They pop up right in front of you!"

"Th-those things are bad news!" Sally wailed, not letting go and pointing wildly at nothing.

"As long as the throne is up, all they can do is touch us. Don't worry!"

"Urgh..."

"Bad news is that I don't think I actually beat it. That thing'll probably be back soon... Oops, there it is. And it brought a friend!"

The ghosts came wafting closer, wailing.

"Time to exorcise!" Maple said, banishing them once more.

Sally was too busy wrapping her head in her scarf to pay much attention.

Not too long after, Maple spotted a run-down mansion below.

The fog was thicker here, so thick that the building was impossible to make out in its entirety.

"Sally! We're here...probably. Double-check?"

"Any ghosts?"

Maple quickly scanned the area.

"Um...not right now! Coast is clear."

Sally tugged the scarf, opening a tiny crack to look through.

"Mm, we're good, that's definitely the place. Okay...let's do this!"

"Coming in for a landing!"

Maple had Syrup slowly descend. Once they were on the

ground, she took Sally's hand again and helped her climb off. Then she put her throne away and returned Syrup to normal size.

Their destination didn't look roomy enough to accommodate a giant Syrup.

Sally fixed her scarf once she realized exploring like that wouldn't be very practical.

"The moment I lose my nerve even once, it'll all be over. Gotta empty out my head. No thoughts at all."

"We going, Sally?"

"W-wait, I'm not ready—"

"I've heard that one before, so I'm just gonna go ahead and be the bad guy."

Not only had Sally made her wait outside a haunted house for a full hour once, that had actually ended with Sally running away, tears in her eyes.

This time, though, Maple was bristling with artillery.

To keep Sally from turning tail, Maple used her self-destruct technique to propel them right at the half-open front doors.

She knew Sally well. Forcing the issue would ultimately be to her benefit.

"Let's make an explosive entrance!"

"Aiiiiieeeee!"

With a boom, they shot through the doors.

As Maple and Sally touched down, the doors slammed shut behind them.

"Come on, Sally! On your feet! You're here for a reason, right?"

"Uh…right. Maple…don't let go."

"You got it!"

Maple took Sally's hand, pulled her up, and then looked around.

The mansion was clearly massive. They were standing in an entrance hall and could see three sets of doors: one in front and one on either side.

There was also a staircase going up and more doors at the top.

The remains of a chandelier hung from the rafters, while the walls were decorated with candelabra, tiny flames clinging to nearly spent candles.

"This place is huge! Where do we go?" Maple asked.

"We should… Oh, wait. I don't actually know."

Sally had looked into it, but there were gaps in her knowledge.

It wasn't that the knowledge wasn't out there—she'd been struggling with simply reading the guides at all.

"In that case, we'll just have to check out everything!" Maple said.

Sally desperately shook her head. "Let's come back when I've looked up where we need to go. That'll be better. Searching without a plan is so inefficient. Plus, the monsters here are pretty tough. We don't want to fight too much. Better that we know the shortest…"

Sally trailed off. Maple was looking at her hard, boring right through Sally's bluster.

"I don't think so," she said, brooking no argument. "Let's just get this over with. You've got me with you, so it'll be *fine*."

"Mm…"

Maple still had Martyr's Devotion active, which blocked basically all attacks.

Accepting that they wouldn't be leaving, Sally managed a few shaky steps, walking like a newborn deer. It didn't look like she'd be much help.

"My hunch says…right!"

Maple moved over to the corresponding door and flung it open.

This kicked up a cloud of dust, but through the opening, they saw a corridor leading away.

Maple put a hand to one ear, listening close, but couldn't hear anything.

"Looks like."

She headed down the hall.

There were paths forking to the left at regular intervals.

And between them, doors that led to even more rooms. There was no shortage of places to search.

"Where do we even start— Wagh!"

Feeling something odd underfoot, Maple looked down.

Countless white hands were reaching up from the floor, grabbing at their ankles and steadily climbing up their legs. To top it all off, the ghost woman they'd met on the way here came right through the wall, heading straight at them.

"M—! M-M-M-M-Maple!"

"Hold on!"

Maple switched her war gear to sword mode. The short sword in her right hand became a giant blade she used to slash at their feet.

Once again, she didn't slay anything, but the hands did vanish.

After their feet were freed, she deployed her artillery again, firing multiple rounds through the persistent apparition.

"Whew. All clear! You good now?"

"Mm. I'm so glad you're here, Maple," Sally murmured. Her spirit already seemed half-broken.

Like Sally had said, the moment she lost her nerve, this little adventure would be over.

"Let's find this stuff quick so we can leave!" After boldly announcing this, Maple was about to take a step right as she noticed a dull blue glow at their feet.

Sally would normally have had no problem getting herself and Maple out of the way.

But not today.

The light steadily grew brighter, and before they knew it, they were somewhere else.

Even before the shining faded, alarms rang in Sally's brain, telling her things she'd really rather not focus on.

Like that Maple's hand was no longer holding hers.

Sally opened her eyes as her regular vision returned. She found herself in a totally different corridor.

"M-Maple? Wh-where are... Eeek!"

Voice shaking, Sally called out—just before a hand landed on her shoulder.

She flinched. Her back bolt upright, she stayed perfectly still as her eyes snapped to the left.

The hand on her shoulder was pale. Far too pale to belong to one of the living.

Sally opened her eyes wide, scared stiff, right as a pair of thin, cold arms wrapped around her.

"Ah...ah! Ah! Aiiiiiieeeee!!"

Screaming, she ran off, easily slipping away from the unknown person's grasp.

Her flight sent her into the nearest room.

"Haah, haah, haah... T-time to log out..."

She pulled up her menu to do just that, only to discover red palms covering it, banging loudly.

"Uaaagh..."

This actually forced her to calm down somewhat.

She regained enough composure to remember there were

certain areas that prevented players from logging out—and exactly what kind of monsters tended to populate those locations.

It was common for enemies in these places to lower AGI every time they grabbed a player—and once their victims' AGI hit zero, they started using instant death moves.

But these areas were always easy to get out of as long as you kept moving.

"Th-they're after me…!"

Sally wasn't dead yet. If she kept moving around the mansion interior, not many spooky things could lay a finger on her.

But clearly, that didn't make it any easier.

◆□◆□◆□◆□◆

Like Sally, Maple found herself suddenly somewhere else.

"Um…Sally?"

A quick scan of her new surroundings revealed no signs of her friend.

She was inside a room.

There was a yawning closet with no door and a dust-laden bed. The sheets were rags, and the floor had seen better days.

"I've gotta find her!"

She grabbed the doorknob to take her leave, but it just rattled in place. The door wouldn't budge.

No keyhole that she could see. In fact, there was no visible reason why it wouldn't open.

"Hmm…dang it. Can I break it down? Might as well try."

Maple pointed her cannon at the door.

Then she heard a creak behind her and spun around.

A shadow was rising off the floor, like the night itself was taking shape.

"Yikes! Heaven's Throne!"

Maple hastily summoned her throne and dived onto it.

"I don't have eyes in the back of my head like Sally, but this helps!"

She watched the shadow closely.

It was vaguely human shaped and was reaching toward her with its hands—but nothing happened.

"Huh. I guess I don't need to worry. Commence Assault!"

Maple fired some rounds, but they all passed right through her target, hitting the wall behind it.

"Hmm. Physical attacks aren't really doing anything... I wonder if beating this thing opens the door? Hmm. Well, let's try!"

Maple leaned forward, sticking her head inside the shadow's torso.

She tried biting, but only got air.

"Nothing's working! Hmm. Oh, I know!"

A moment of inspiration later, she quickly started searching through her inventory.

She still had some of those papers left—the ones she'd used to poke the King of Light's toes.

Fire and wind hadn't been effective against that boss, so she still had heaps of them left.

"Starting a fire here would be scary, so let's go with wind. Take that!"

When she used the item, a gust of wind tore through the room, shredding the shadow.

"Nice, it worked! Don't believe me? Here, have another!"

She started sticking more papers on it.

The shadow was only a bit smaller than your average trash mob, and it went down after the tenth item.

Since these items were only usable at ultra-close range and took no skill at all, not many players bothered using them. As a result, the damage they dealt was surprisingly respectable.

When the shadow faded away, Maple heard the door behind her click.

"So it *was* locked! Even though it didn't have a keyhole..."

She put her throne away and tried the knob again.

This time the door opened easily.

"Yes! I'm free!"

She quickly left before the room decided to trap her again.

"Let's look for Sally. Gonna keep an eye on the floor this time. Last thing I want is to get teleported again."

Maple plodded off down the corridor.

◆□◆□◆□◆□◆

By this time, Sally was shivering under a desk in a room she'd stumbled into.

She couldn't bring herself to go out, so she'd decided to wait for Maple.

"O-oh...I could send her a message..."

She did exactly that.

All she wrote was that she couldn't log out and needed rescuing. Nothing that would actually improve her situation was included, but she was too far gone to realize that.

"I'll just stay here for a few more minutes," Sally whispered.

By that she meant "until Maple gets here."

Or possibly "forever."

But this area was not about to let *that* happen.

The door opened with a creak.

Sally couldn't see it from her hiding spot, but she heard something step in.

She clapped her hands over her mouth, holding her breath.

Warped floorboards creaked.

A few moments after hearing that, Sally saw pale feet appear right in front of her. They clearly didn't belong to anything alive.

"......!!"

She prayed for them to pass on by, and perhaps her prayers were answered because the feet kept walking.

".........."

But just as relief washed over her, there was a beep—message received.

Maple was *nice*. She *always* answered. But the noise startled Sally, and she banged her head on the desk.

The feet swung back toward her, and Sally somersaulted out from the desk, scrambling out the door.

"Maple! Maplllle! Heeeeelp!"

But the only answer to her screams was grasping hands reaching out from the walls and the ghosts of blood-soaked, maimed children.

"Superspeed! *Superspeed! Superspeed!*"

Sally ran like hell into another room.

But this mansion was *full* of ghosts. There was no way to escape them.

Thoroughly lost, Sally was running mindlessly—and heading deeper inside.

"Hic...sniff..."

She ran and ran, from room to room.

Cold hands kept grabbing at her.

She was way past being able to just run away.

If these ghosts had looked like orcs and goblins, Sally could easily have dodged right through their midst without letting even a finger touch her.

But if her special flair didn't kick in, stats-wise, she was nothing more than a slightly more nimble than average player.

And Sally's AGI was down to a quarter of its full value.

Any change in stats could tank her dodging skills, so it was no wonder she was getting swiped at left and right.

This soon proved too much for her, and Sally holed up in a closet, eyes closed tight, shaking like a leaf.

She sent Maple a message saying she was in a closet and specified that she didn't need a reply. She'd completely given up on surviving this solo.

"Maple...*sniff*...get here soon..."

Sally whispered through her sniffles, but no answer came.

Two figures were slowly converging on Sally's location.

One was the ghost that had been chasing her, and the other was Maple, who'd finally made it to the same floor.

This was pure coincidence—Maple was just systematically searching every single room.

"Where in the world is Sally...? I've searched a *lot* of rooms now...but at least she's still not dead!"

Since they were in a party, she could see Sally's status and, more importantly, her approximate location. She was clearly still inside the haunted house.

Maple was plastering her items on every ghost she found like a Shinto priest exorcising spirits with paper talismans.

A bloodstained ghost child appeared before her, coming her way.

"Oof... Go into that white light— Wah?!"

Maple had opened her inventory but found her screen covered in red handprints.

"Man, that caught me by surprise! Um…items, items…"

She didn't really let it get to her. She soon slapped a paper charm on the ghostly child.

It caught fire and quietly faded away.

Maple looked back at her inventory to ready another charm.

Then she realized she couldn't log out. After moving around a bit, she found the threshold of the zone that prevented her from logging out.

"So this is what Sally was talking about. Does that mean she's nearby?"

This was her first real sign of progress. Maple pumped a fist.

"But…how is she holding up?"

The ghosts here seemed significantly scarier than anything she'd come across earlier, and Maple did not think Sally could handle them well at all.

"Yeah, she'll be a mess for sure. I'd better find her quick."

The corridor looked ominous, so Maple kept her shield up, moving cautiously forward.

"Sally…probably won't answer if I call. But she's definitely crying…"

Maple did her best to prick up her ears, trying to catch the sound of Sally's sniffles. She checked every inch of every room.

"Oh, right! I should tell her I'm close."

Maple sent Sally a quick message, then resumed her search.

Maple's message reached Sally.

Sally read it, and her face lit up. It was like a ray of hope had shone upon it.

"Oh! Footsteps…! Maple?"

Whoever was coming closer stopped outside the room. Then she heard the door open.

Sally was hiding in a closet to the right of that door.

"Just a peek…"

Sally cracked the closet door, looking to see who'd come in.

The message that had arrived moments before made her certain this was Maple.

And her desperate need for salvation led to this lapse in judgment.

Long spindly arms. Sallow skin. An unrecognizable face, but the long hair hanging over it failed to disguise the empty eye sockets or the tears of blood flowing from those twin black pits.

In that instant, Sally knew.

It had *seen* her.

"Eep……!"

She slammed the closet door shut but heard the floorboards creak right outside.

"No, no, no!"

Sally held the door shut, but her hands were shaking too hard, and it was overpowering her.

The ghost's empty eye sockets locked on her through the gap in the door.

"Ah…!"

Sally went limp, collapsing in a heap on the closet floor.

The door was flung open wide, and the ghost's hand reached for her.

Black shadows spilled out from the horrifying creature, and blood seeped from its eye sockets.

"I'm sorry...I'm sorry...!"

"Heaven's Throne!"

Just as Sally abandoned all hope, Maple leaped through the open door. Seeing Sally's predicament, she hastily pulled out her throne and sat down upon it.

A circle of light spread out beneath the ghost's feet, dispelling the sinister curtain of shadows.

"Sally, you okay?"

"Unh...unghhh...Maplllle...!"

Sally scrambled out of the closet, clinging to Maple on her throne.

"Whew! But now what?"

Maple looked up and found the ghost hovering over them. The ominous shadows might be gone, but even Maple thought this thing was creepy.

"It's hella staring at us..."

Maple averted her eyes, trying to push its face away with both hands only to find them passing right through it.

"Augh...urgh...wahh..."

"Seriously, now what?"

Maple was stuck sitting down, at a total loss.

CHAPTER 4

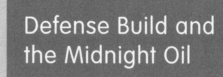

Defense Build and the Midnight Oil

Maple sat on her throne awhile with the ghost glaring at her, but eventually having Maple with her made Sally calm down.

"Maple...is it still there?" she asked, not daring to look herself.

"Yeah, it is."

"Gah...why won't it just go away?"

Sally's voice was still shaking, but she sounded a lot more like herself.

"Feeling better?"

"A bit, yeah. Don't look. I'm sure I look hideous."

Maple had already gotten an eyeful of Sally's tearstained expression.

Besides, there was no hiding how red her ears were. Maple could imagine everything else was the same color.

"Sure, sure. Was this thing really worth all this?"

"Honestly, even I don't know anymore. I want to punch myself for ever thinking I could handle this."

Sally admitted the skills and items that were up for grabs had prevented her from seeing the truth.

"It isn't every day you misjudge this badly."

"There were just too many skills I wanted. But I'm done! I've calmed down, I'm thinking straight, and I can definitely make do without these skills."

"So what skill was it you wanted?" Maple asked. "You didn't actually tell me."

Sally began explaining all the skills and items that had tempted her and everything she'd read about that was going down around the map.

"What do you think? If we're careful not to get separated again, we could search some more."

"Th-the skill here doesn't matter anymore. I...just wanna leave."

"Gotcha! That said...hrmm."

Maple had been rather hoping the ghost would go away while they talked, but apparently it was quite persistent.

"We can't risk leaving the throne... Maybe we can attack from here?"

Maple reached out, using one of her items to shoot razor-sharp slices of wind at the ghost.

It staggered backward.

Problem was, it had no HP bar. Maple knew full well that meant this thing didn't take damage and couldn't be defeated.

It moaned, clutching its face in both hands. But not long after, it came toward them again, reaching out.

"We could try running while it recoils... Think you can manage, Sally? I bet it would catch up with me."

Of course, that meant Sally would have to leave Maple behind.

"Um...nope. Not happening."

And this was clearly not *just* because her AGI was now at zero.

"Then what should...huh?"

After all that hovering, the ghost had suddenly drifted away from them, leaving the room.

Maple just gaped after it, astonished.

"Now's our chance!" she said. "Come on, Sally!"

"Huh? What? O-oh…!"

Sally had been too busy staring at the floor to notice, but when Maple pulled her hand, she lurched into motion.

For the first time ever, their running speeds were evenly matched.

From behind them, they heard yowls—likely the ghost's *new* victims.

Sally knew her screams of horror must have been just as blood-curdling, and her face started turning red.

"We're out!"

Maple had taken the shortest route she knew out of the no-logout zone.

"Thanks, Maple."

"Eh-heh-heh… You're welcome!"

But even as they rejoiced, cold hands wrapped around them from behind.

"Eek……!"

"Hng!"

They froze to the spot—and earned a skill.

"Um…Nether Nexus? Oh, the skill that doubles an item's effect."

Maple checked the description.

Sally was too busy collapsing in a heap to be curious, but she'd earned the same skill.

The flavor text suggested they had earned themselves an uncanny ally that would occasionally reach out from behind, lending a helping hand.

"Ughhh…I *so* don't need anything like that…"

This was the skill Sally had been after, but she did not look pleased.

"What do you think? I'm up for more if you are."

"I'm logging out," Sally said, not even tempted. "Gotta get home."

"I figured. Bye, then!"

Maple waved.

"Thanks for helping, though. I'll make it up to you eventually."

"No prob. You've helped me more than enough already! I finally got to pay you back a bit."

Maple grinned, and for the first time, Sally regained some of her old cheer.

"Well, thanks anyway. See you when the seventh stratum exists."

"I bet you come back before then."

"I won't! I've learned my lesson!"

With a feeble smile, Sally logged out.

Back in the real world, Risa got out of bed and put her console away.

"Ugh, I'm soaked with sweat. Gotta hit the bath… No, not yet. I should eat first."

She opened the door a *tad* more quietly than usual and went downstairs.

Her mother was in the living room, getting dinner ready.

"Risa? Food's not ready yet."

"Mm, just gonna watch TV, then."

Risa grabbed the remote and flopped down on the couch.

There was nothing on, and she wound up just channel surfing.

While she was killing time before dinner, the phone rang.

Risa twisted on the couch, looking toward the sound.

"Oh…yes, Shiromine speaking. That's right."

"…………"

Her mother kept talking for a while and finally put the phone down.

"Risa, something's come up. I've gotta run. And your dad'll be back late tonight—you better eat before the food gets cold."

"Oh…a-all right."

Oblivious to Risa's unease, her mother hustled off to get ready.

"I'll be back as soon as I can!"

"…Got it."

And with that, her mother left.

It was already dark out. The only sound in the house came from the TV.

"I-I'd better eat!"

Risa had gone to the door to see her mother off. She made a beeline for the dining table and started dinner.

"……"

She picked up the remote again, upping the volume.

As she ate, her feet kept twitching. Her eyes were somewhat pinched.

Her chopsticks made slow progress.

When her plate was finally clean, she took the dishes to the sink and started channel surfing again.

The weather report promised rain that evening.

She frittered away the time, but nobody came home.

"I *do* need a bath…but…"

Risa's heart was racing. She couldn't settle down.

And she knew exactly why.

"I'm just…spooked."

And saying it out loud made it worse.

Risa made sure all the curtains were closed, then hugged a couch cushion tight, making herself very small.

"Oh!"

She'd had an idea that made her brighten right up.

Meanwhile, Kaede was busy studying—she'd logged out shortly after Risa.

Her phone rang.

"Is that…? I thought so."

Kaede picked up her phone to find Risa calling.

"Hello?"

"Oh, Kaede? Got a sec?"

"Mm, sure, what's up?"

"I was just thinking I was a real headache today. Can we talk a bit?"

Kaede had a pretty good idea why Risa was *really* calling, but she left that unsaid. They chatted away like they always did.

"Mm?"

But as they talked, Kaede started hearing water running.

"Is she taking a bath? That *would* scare her… Oops!"

Kaede realized she'd said that out loud.

Risa must have decided to pretend she hadn't heard anything, but that did leave an awkward silence.

"R-Risa?"

It took a moment, but eventually Risa said, "Kaede, thing is… there's nobody else home."

"Uh-huh."

"So…I was just feeling a little jittery…"

"Mm-hmm."

"Or, I guess, scared. Do you mind keeping me company?"

Kaede was hardly about to say no here, so they kept talking.

And as they talked, Kaede remembered that this wasn't the first time.

"You've done this before, right?"

"Have I?"

"Yeah, although you didn't call me from the bath that time. But I sure didn't get much sleep that night…"

"Oh, back in grade school? Ugh, I haven't grown up at *all*."

But talking like this certainly seemed to be helping her nerves.

She got out of the bath, and the discussion only heated up. By the time she was ready to turn in, Risa seemed much more herself.

"Good night, Risa."

"Mm. Thanks. Good night, Kaede."

Risa would usually have stayed up a few hours longer.

But instead, she turned out the lights and burrowed under her covers.

She could hear it raining outside.

Going to bed this early wasn't really helping her sleep.

Half an hour passed. An hour.

And as time passed, her fears came rising back up.

"Mm…hngg…"

She rolled back and forth awhile but finally gave up and reached for her phone.

There was only one person she could call at times like this.

As her ring yanked Kaede out of her slumber, Risa got up and flipped on the lights.

"Ah-ha-ha… You've done *this* before, too."

"I'm so sorry, Kaede… Really, I am…"

Needless to say, the next day Kaede had trouble staying awake.

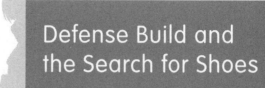

CHAPTER 5

Defense Build and the Search for Shoes

A few days after Maple and Sally got lost in the haunted house...

Maple was hanging out alone in the Guild Home. Sally had not yet been foolish enough to consider another run at the map of terror.

"Sally's busy grinding on the fifth stratum while Mai and Yui are exploring on other levels, too... What should I do?"

The twins were struggling with the sixth stratum for very different reasons.

Most monsters here were immune to physical attacks, which meant their normally deadly blows were not so helpful.

"Hmm, you know, one thing Sally wanted was actually equipment."

Maple nodded to herself and decided to go find that for her.

"I promised she could have anything I found that would help her build, but I never actually found anything! This'll be perfect."

Sally had given her an accessory that boosted her HP and helped a lot when she was gathering crafting materials. *And* Sally had been the one who earned all the gold they needed to purchase the Guild Home.

Maple thought it was high time she returned the favor.

"But Sally said she hadn't actually looked up where to get them…"

Sally had been so busy freaking out that her information gathering had been…selective. So Maple would have to start by checking the bulletin board in the town square.

"Time to head on out!"

She departed the Guild Home with some pep in her step.

At the end of a long road lined with abandoned houses, she found the information boards.

"Wow, so many people…"

The stratum was still brand new, and lots of people were scoping out the boards.

Maple wriggled her tiny frame through the wave of humanity until she could see well enough to scan for the intel she sought.

"Hmm…there! That's it!"

Maple made sure she knew the location and the success conditions. As she pushed her way back out of the crowd, she ran into some familiar faces—Pain, Dread, and Drag from the Order of the Holy Sword.

"Oh, Pain! You guys are looking for info, too?"

"More or less. Gotta keep up with you, Maple."

"He's all fired up for a rematch! So am I, for that matter."

"Eh-heh-heh! Well, I'll try not to disappoint."

"…Uh, hey, Frederica's been looking for Sally. Griping that she can't find her for another duel," Drag said.

Maple smiled awkwardly, unable to admit the truth. She wound up promising to pass word along.

*   *   *

After they parted ways, Maple pushed her way farther out. Finally, she escaped and breathed a sigh of relief.

"It might be pretty crowded in the fields, too..."

That was a concern, but it didn't stop her hopping aboard Syrup and flying away.

"Tons of people here, just as I expected."

Maple looked down and saw the sparkle and shine of skills and spells below.

The monsters here were all undead, made entirely of gleaming white bones.

They tended to vanish and reappear, evading attacks, and of course—they were immune to physical damage.

"Oof, that makes it hard for me."

Most of Maple's skills were wide-area attacks or close-range strikes, and she honestly didn't have anything that was geared toward carefully aiming at significant range.

"I wonder if they show up anywhere else?"

Maple decided to skip this location and search elsewhere.

Fortunately, the target monsters had a glow to them that was relatively easy to spot from above, so her plan seemed reasonable.

"If I don't see any, I can always come back. Let's go with that. Syrup, onward!"

She had her pet swing round so they could set out, going farther and farther from the town.

"Nothing? Well, let's just keep looking."

Maple was peering over the edge of Syrup's shell, keeping a close watch on the ground.

Not long after, the fog thickened as they neared the mountains.

"Now I can't see anything... Maybe I should check the peak? That's where I'd hide stuff!"

She had Syrup fly lower, landing in an open area.

"Thanks, Syrup!"

She made her pet turtle-size again before starting her ascent.

Not long after, she ran into a monster made of red bones shrouded in the mist.

"Not quite the right color...but maybe it'll work!"

Clearly a *different* monster, so not really what she was after, but Maple decided to beat it anyway.

"Okay! Taunt! You aren't getting away from me!"

Using Taunt actually made several more of the same monster close in.

"Nice! Luck is on my side."

It always took Maple a while to find enemies, so she never objected to them coming after her.

"Hydra!"

This hadn't been an option at the haunted house.

Poison gushed out of the magic circle, swallowing up the monsters.

"Whaa...? They survived *that*?!"

Apparently, they boasted high poison resistance, given that one Hydra was not enough to take them down.

Maple had not been expecting them to be this tough.

Black smoke rose from the monsters' backs, forming the shapes of skulls.

An earsplitting shriek went up from the bones below.

"W-wait...that looks like bad news! Heaven's Throne!"

Maple flopped onto the throne like it was an emergency escape.

It worked—Heaven's Throne sealed Attribute: Evil attacks, and it was clearly canceling the smoke skulls.

"Mm, but if I'm sitting down, I can't attack, either. It's pretty, so I *want* to use it more, but..."

All these physically resistant monsters were making fights longer, too. Maple tended to struggle when Machine God didn't work.

"If I was with someone... Argh, I miss Sally. Hngg...I'm doing this for her, too..."

The whole point was to explore the sixth stratum where Sally couldn't.

If she could find the shoes Sally wanted, it might cheer her up. She *had* to make this work.

Once again, Maple fell back on the paper charms.

"I'll have to restock," Maple muttered, burning the face off a spirit. "Wait, I think I saw some exorcism charms for sale, too. Maybe I should get those instead?"

"Boom!"

The last of the red ghouls vanished, dropping materials.

"Hmm...not what I was after. I don't even know if these guys drop it..."

It was easier for Maple to fight when no one else was around, so she had definitely been hoping these would drop the shoes, too.

But they weren't the monster the board posts had mentioned, so her efforts would likely be in vain.

"Maybe I can get something else Sally would like... At the least, I can give these materials to Iz. She's always looking after my equipment!"

And grinding here would help Maple raise her level.

She hadn't spent much time fighting recently, so maybe it was high time she did.

Maple remained perched on her throne, eyes gleaming as she looked for any new red ghouls.

"Oh, there's one! There's always a lot of these, huh?"

The red ghoul drew close before launching a magic attack at her.

"Oh, they have normal spells?"

Red light hit Maple in the guts and burst loudly, vanishing.

"Nice! No damage! Come on, now, just a little closer...!"

Maple beckoned to the red ghoul, and when it came into range, she slapped a fire charm on it.

"This sure takes a while. I've been mowing foes down lately, so this really takes me back."

But a leisurely fight was a nice change of pace, and Maple wasn't exactly stressing out about it.

"Clear! Oh, the next guy's here."

Maple smiled, waving it toward her.

That red ghoul was clearly neither "guy" nor human, but it lunged right at her, its attacks uselessly whiffing. It was soon vanquished.

"Oh, right. Don't my poison skills have an instant death effect now? This skill!"

She'd nearly forgotten all about that.

This was the skill she'd learned by beating all the monsters in the pot on the fourth stratum.

Bug Urn Curse

Applies a 10% instant death chance to all poison attacks.
This is unaffected by poison resistance skills.

"Hmm, so if I use weaker skills, the instant death effect might

kick in? I'm running low on attack items, so it's worth a shot! Um...
Venom Cutter!"

Multiple red ghouls were approaching, and these poison blades
were nowhere near as powerful as Hydra—but if the instant death
kicked in, that wouldn't matter. Unfortunately, the ghouls looked
totally unfazed.

"No luck, huh? And I'll end up needing MP potions soon. Man,
fighting solo is hard."

But given everything Sally had done for Maple, one pair of
shoes would hardly be enough.

"I've gotta play for the both of us on this stratum... Yeah, I
like the sound of that. I'm sure she'll be thrilled to get a bunch of
presents."

Maple tried the poison thing a few more times, then had a horrifying thought.

"Wait... Are you guys *immune* to instant death?!"

She reached out and tried to thump one of them on its rib cage,
but her hand passed right through it.

The ghoul did not seem inclined to answer her question.

And then Maple realized a much more obvious problem.

The throne she was sitting on was fundamentally incompati-
ble with curses.

The name *Bug Urn Curse* even sounded evil.

"Argh! I-is *that* why?! Ugh. This throne is great, but...it's too
effective! Does that mean I'm stuck using items, then? Or do I have
to ask for help?"

Maple decided to fight until she ran out of items, and once her
stock was gone, she ran away before any more red ghouls found her.

"Syrup, take us home. Next time we'll have to do better."

She gave the ground below a baleful glare, vowing to return
soon as she flew back to town.

◆□◆□◆□◆□◆

When she arrived, she had Syrup take her in for a landing.

"Whew...there should be a bunch of items that work on some spooky boys!"

She'd seen some before, and she was certain they weren't the only ones. She set off down the street.

"Let's hit up the shop with the exorcism charms first."

She went inside, ready to stock up.

"I think they were...yeah, right here."

The charms were made of paper, with indecipherable characters written on them in red ink.

Maple double-checked the item name, making sure these were exorcism charms, then bought as many as she could.

"Maybe I should sell these materials? I'm running low on money."

She was planning on checking other stores and doing more shopping, so she sold all the extra materials she'd collected on this stratum, making her wallet flush again.

Deciding nothing else here was immediately useful, Maple left the shop and headed off down the main road.

There were shops on both sides of the street, all looking rather worse for wear.

"How do I find the good stuff?" Maple wondered, head swiveling back and forth—then she saw a familiar face coming her way. "Oh! Mii!"

Maple waved, and Mii came over.

Talking quietly so no one else could hear, Mii asked, "How's it been, Maple? Enjoying the new stratum?"

"It's not bad. I'm looking for items that work on ghosts. My attacks aren't really good for that."

"Check the place at the dead end here. They had Banishing Salts, I think? Something like that anyway."

Maple's face lit up. "Thanks! I'll take a look."

"Mm. Hope it helps."

"Lemme know if you need anything, I'll come running."

Mii gave Maple a wave and continued on her merry way.

Maple watched her go, then headed for the shop she'd mentioned.

She didn't have to walk for long.

The previous shops had all been run down, but this one had intact windows. It looked surprisingly normal for this area.

"Um…is this the exorcist shop? Looks like it!"

Relieved, Maple stepped inside.

It had row after row of items and accessories.

A much bigger selection than Maple had imagined. She headed right toward the accessory section.

"They even have shields and short swords! Um, Purging Great Shield and Purging Short Sword, hmm."

The short sword had a bonus to attack damage against ghost-type monsters.

And the great shield reduced incoming damage from that same type.

"Hmm…but that won't help me."

She put them back on the shelf.

Maple didn't really take damage to begin with, so the shield was useless.

And since she couldn't do type-specific damage, the short sword wouldn't really help her much.

"I guess it's just the Banishing Salts, then. I'll buy some of those."

She looked around and found the salts in the item section.

She bought them and then stocked up on the fire and wind charms she'd been using.

"That oughtta be...hmm?"

Maple had glanced around to make sure she hadn't missed anything, which was how she spotted something in the corner she'd totally overlooked.

"Um, a vacuum cleaner?"

It was certainly shaped like one. Maple ran her fingers down the nozzle of the extension.

The device sported the same red writing as the charms, and this shop was heavily specialized, so the item clearly came imbued with some sort of exorcism effect. She picked it up.

"Hmm, could I use this? Oh, no. This is like those fermentation weights."

It was just a decorative item for your room. Maple put it back down and left.

On the street outside, she muttered, "This would be a lot easier if you could just suck 'em up with a vacuum cleaner... I wish that thing worked."

But no matter how much she wished for it, the words *room decoration* were still undeniably in the vacuum cleaner's description.

CHAPTER 6

Defense Build and Exorcism

A few days later, Maple was back in the misty mountains.

"Bring it on!"

She landed, made Syrup small, and started looking for red ghouls.

"There they are!"

She immediately used Taunt, and once they started converging on her, she summoned her throne, sealing the ghosts' skills.

"This time I've got the good charms! Ker-splat!"

She stuck one of the exorcism charms to it, and the red writing glowed bright. A white halo appeared around the ghoul.

The glowing monster's HP began to drop, and it let out a hideous wail.

"Oh, it's working! Have some salt, too!"

Maple sprinkled some Banishment Salts on it, and another chunk of HP vanished.

When the HP bar was drained, the ghost stayed wreathed in white light, gently rising up toward the heavens.

"And it's exorcised! These materials…do a pretty bang-up job! Ugh, wait, did I not get any XP?!"

Exorcising these ghosts sacrificed experience gains for an improved item drop rate—plus it was much faster and easier than fighting them normally.

Maple debated which was better for a moment but could not resist how convenient it was to just sit back throwing salt and charms.

"Let's just kill a bunch of them and see what happens. Seems like they do drop some items anyway!"

She tossed a handful of salt at another ghoul, racking up the damage.

"I like it!"

Maple started exorcising every ghost that came in range.

It didn't take much to defeat these things, and she had plenty of stock in her inventory.

After a solid two hours of exorcism, Maple left the mountain behind.

"Sally likes to hit the same group of monsters multiple times to get the stuff she needs, but I gotta say it's not much fun."

But she was doing this for Sally, so she wasn't giving up easy.

She kept doing exorcism runs for the next few days, until it started to seem like she must have exorcised every ghost on this mountain. And at long last—a pair of shoes dropped.

"Yesssss! Finally!"

Maple scooped them up the moment she saw them.

They had some dark red stains on them and felt oddly cold to the touch, but they were shaped more or less like the boots Sally already wore.

"They're called…Charnel Boots? Wow, that sounds cursed. Are they safe to wear? It says they're rare, so they must be."

Maple inspected them carefully, but they weren't oozing blood or anything, and she couldn't find any bits of stray flesh left inside, either.

"Mm, I think I can safely give these to Sally. Let's check this skill, though…"

One Step in the Grave

When skill is active, makes a foothold in midair at the cost of a −5 penalty to all stats.
Penalty lasts twenty minutes.
Foothold vanishes in ten seconds.

"Hmm…that isn't quite what I'd heard. I guess I'll just have to see what Sally thinks."

She put the shoes in her inventory and saw a ghost coming her way. She decided this would be her last battle.

"Salt and charm ready… Wait…"

Maple was braced to exorcise it, but this ghost wasn't like the others.

It was glowing blue, not red, and actually kept its distance from her.

Maple squinted as she followed it with her eyes and saw it stop not too far away.

Its light flickered, as if it was calling to her.

"Worth a shot. Just gotta put my throne away… All right, let's check it out."

She kept her shield up, just in case, and began following the blue light.

When she got close, the ghost moved again, as if leading her on.

"Up the mountain, huh? Welp, let's see where it takes me!"

*   *   *

The ghost led Maple higher and higher, all the way to the peak.

The fog was extra thick up here; Maple couldn't see more than a yard in any direction.

"I just keep going? Oh no..."

Her foot had bumped something. It turned out to be an old wooden cross stuck in the ground.

Nearby she saw the remains of a weather-beaten bouquet.

"D-did I kick those? I'm so sorry!"

Maple closed her eyes, clapping her palms together.

Then a pale hand shot out of the ground and grabbed Maple's ankle.

"Hnyaah?! Hey! Let go!"

The hand pulled on her foot—and then she suddenly found herself floating in midair, as if the ground beneath her feet had been an illusion all along.

She fell so long she wound up screwing her eyes closed.

When that feeling finally went away, she found herself in darkness.

"Um, where have I been sent *this* time?"

She looked around—and red lights appeared in the darkness.

A monster appeared, as if clawing its way through a crack in space. It looked like a giant version of the red ghouls Maple had exorcised hundreds of.

Only the top half made it through the fissure, but those red arms were several times as long as Maple was tall.

"Wh-wh-what now?"

One look at it was enough to convince Maple she wasn't exorcising this anytime soon.

But it didn't seem inclined to let her leave. It was already reaching out, trying to grab her.

"Whoa...mm? It's...surprisingly slow?"

Maple ran and easily made it out of reach.

This was essentially the first time Maple had ever successfully run away from an enemy. She was so shocked she stopped and looked it over once more.

The ghostly arm disappeared, and the crack in space closed up.

"Oh, that can't be good... Agh, I knew it!"

She'd spun around, and she found the crack opening right in front of her.

"How about some *salt* instead!"

Maple threw a handful of salt at the emerging upper body, ran quickly out of range, and then checked the damage.

"Woo, it worked!"

The salt wasn't as effective as it had been on the ghouls outside, but it had definitely taken a chunk of the ghost's HP.

Figuring this might work out, she took all the items out of her inventory and started throwing them with wild abandon.

"Take that! Come on...hnggg?!"

Her eyes had locked on the rift.

Between the sides of the rift and the boss ghoul stood several smaller red ghosts.

And just like the ones outside, they had ominous-looking skulls hovering over them.

"Stay back! Heaven's Throne!"

She quickly sat down, canceling out the ghosts' skills.

But sitting down made it harder for her to avoid the boss's attacks.

"Still, it's better than trying to run and messing it up."

Maple decided to stay put and let the boss hit where it might. Its hands circled around her.

"Can't use your skill? Then it's my turn!"

She began slapping charms all over the boss's palms, racking up the damage.

Maple was hoping this would exorcise it, but the boss had other plans.

"Uh-oh, it's grabbed me!"

The palms had closed in, picking Maple up.

"Whatever...ow?!"

A shock ran through Maple, and her HP took a hit.

And she could tell her HP was dropping faster than the throne could heal.

"Urgh, piercing attacks!"

It was clearly planning on squeezing her to death.

She struggled, trying to free herself, but to no avail.

And the ghost wasn't done yet.

"Er, wait...nooooo!"

It lifted her up, hoisting her high into the air.

The throne's effect only worked while she was sitting down. Up here, it did absolutely nothing.

"Urgh...owww...l-let go...! Oh! Atrocity!"

If she'd been dragged off her throne, that meant she had access to *all* her skills again.

Monster Maple spawned inside the ghost's grasp, and she easily tore herself free, backing well away from it.

"Ugh, haven't felt pain like that in a long time. I'm getting careless."

Maple hadn't dismissed it, so the throne was still sitting there, and if she sat down, it would activate again.

"But maybe I'd better figure out what this boss can do while Atrocity is still up... Yeah, that sounds like a plan."

Taking damage always made Maple cautious. She decided to watch her foe carefully.

With this monster skin on her, any damage she took wouldn't actually affect her HP. And she felt no pain.

"Okay, okay...gotta remember my own skills... I can do this. Sally drilled the basic theory into me."

She was talking out loud, trying to calm her nerves while keeping a healthy distance from her foe.

It didn't take Maple long to realize nothing she could do in Atrocity form would actually hurt this boss. She looked very annoyed.

"I can breathe fire and take out the little ones, but...argh, I don't *wanna* ditch this body!"

She tried to focus on figuring out the ghost's moves but was dreading going back to her regular form.

Several minutes later, Maple finally stopped running. It was less that she'd gleaned all the information she could and more that she'd finally gritted her teeth and admitted she had to drop Atrocity. The dark form's belly split open, and Maple fell out.

"Let's start with Full Deploy!"

Braced for an emergency evac, she then called out Syrup and made it giant.

"Syrup! Spirit Cannon! Then stay up in the air!"

Maple had not *just* been running around. She'd come up with a *plan*. But it only half worked—when Syrup tried to fly up, darkness descended, forcing it back to the ground.

But Syrup unleashed a beam of white light that pierced the darkness, swallowing up the little ghosts in its path.

"Cool, it works on ghosts! Thanks, Syrup!"

With these piercing attacks threatening her, she couldn't risk using Martyr's Devotion.

She decided to play like a great shielder should, tanking for Syrup.

"Shield: Good! Salt: Good!"

Exorcism item in hand, she used her self-destruct flight to rocket herself into the space Syrup had cleared.

Trailing flames behind her, Maple burst through the darkness, flung a handful of salt on the boss, and came in for a landing.

"Urgh, it's hard to land in the dark..."

Then she flew back to her throne and tumbled onto it.

Syrup lined up alongside it—now they didn't need to worry about the smaller ghouls' skills.

"Whew...right now, it seems like your attack is my best bet, Syrup, so I'll just have to sit tight until you can fire again."

Anytime smaller ghouls got close, she threw items at them.

When the boss reached out to grab her, she exploded on her throne, rocketing herself skyward—her idea of evasive maneuvers.

"Just gotta keep— Syrup!"

Maple had been busy taking out a small ghoul, but when she turned around, she found the boss aiming a piercing attack at her pet.

"Er, uh...Martyr's Devotion!"

There were too many small spooks around for her to leave the chair. Desperate to protect her pet, she acted on impulse.

"Urp...uh...M-Meditation!"

Unless the boss actually picked her up, Meditation and the throne's own healing were enough to restore her health.

And that kept her from defeat, even if it came after Syrup.

Still—even if she could heal from it, Maple objected on principle to taking damage.

"Wagh, it stings!"

Waves of pain were coursing through her.

But all she could do was sit on her throne and wait for the attack to end.

Eventually the boss let up and went back to summoning the smaller minions.

"Syrup, you still there? Ugh. I dunno, though. I can't handle that again."

She theoretically had the stats to survive it, but Maple was vehemently against all forms of pain and didn't appreciate having to endure this attack at all.

If it kept going after Syrup, she'd be in trouble—and that worry led to *inspiration*.

Though perhaps it didn't deserve such a grandiose term.

"Just put Syrup back in the ring, you doofus!"

With Syrup safely stowed away, all the pain vanished. She didn't *need* to keep her pet out all the time!

"I should really make a habit of doing that when Syrup's in trouble. Lesson learned!"

Maple soon refocused on the battle in front of her.

The threat itself had hardly gone away.

As long as it had piercing attacks, she didn't have time to waste thinking about anything else.

"I'm gonna back off and summon Syrup again. This'll be real rough without Spirit Cannon."

She deployed her weapons and made them explode, launching herself as far from the ghouls as possible.

"Hey, buddy, come on out."

She then kept the turtle safe while they waited for the cooldown.

"Syrup, Spirit Cannon!"

From that point on, she had Syrup attack whenever it could,

and in between kept it small and tucked under her arm, using Martyr's Devotion to keep it safe from her explosive flights.

Maple kept playing keep-away, making this one of those rare boss fights in which she actually tried to *avoid* attacks.

"I've done a lot of damage now..."

And that had clearly caused a phase shift.

It had always been dark in here, but she'd still been able to see herself and the boss—so it was about as bright as a moonlit night.

But now giant Syrup was hovering right next to her, and she couldn't see it. Couldn't see her throne, not even the light of Martyr's Devotion on the ground around her—and of course, she could see no ghosts at all.

Maple was shrouded in darkness, like she had her eyes closed.

"Wh-where are you? Syrup!"

She hastily put her pet back in its ring, then hunched over behind her shield, eyes darting in all directions. Frantically trying to glean any information from her surroundings.

"If I can't see it coming...hngg..."

She narrowed her eyes, but she couldn't even see her own hands, so this was obviously no help.

"Oh! I have a lantern."

She pulled the lantern out of her inventory, trying to light her immediate surroundings a bit.

Unfortunately, even that light was swallowed by the darkness, vanishing like a candle in the wind.

"What the...? H-how am I supposed to see?!"

She tried using the lantern again, but with the same results.

"Wh-where is...? Augh!"

A cold hand grabbed her from behind.

This attack robbed her of STR and AGI, but fortunately that did absolutely nothing to Maple.

"Gah, I can't get away!"

On the other hand, since she had no STR, she also couldn't escape the ghost's grasp.

For nearly a minute, the hand gradually carried Maple higher.

"Is it doing damage...? Eek?!"

She'd screwed up her eyes, expecting pain—but none came.

Instead—Maple's HP suddenly dropped to zero. Indomitable Guardian kicked in, and Maple was dropped to the floor.

The fall didn't hurt, but if she took damage again, she was done for.

"Uh, what in the...? Wh-wh-what do I do...?!"

She was at a loss, but she knew one thing for sure—she couldn't let it use that attack a second time.

"M-my throne! Where did it go?!"

She started running, fully aware her throne was still out there somewhere.

If she put it away, there was a lengthy cooldown before she could use it again, so that wasn't an option.

This was Maple, though—she hadn't actually thought that through. She was just running away from the immediate threat.

"I can't find it anywhere!"

Sensing something coming up behind her, she started to serpentine.

She was gradually getting her wits back, remembering other options.

She considered rocketing away, but since she couldn't see where her opponent was, that might lead to her just rocketing right into it. Maple decided the risk wasn't worth it.

That left her with no option but sprinting senselessly and, every so often, feeling a chilly draft at her back that left her very pale.

She was starting to run out of breath, too. She decided to go with her only other idea.

"How's Syrup doing...? Good, Spirit Cannon's primed. In which case...let's put the throne away."

But just as she was certain she'd improved her predicament, something caught her legs.

"Huh...?"

She looked down and saw white hands reaching out of the ground, wrapping themselves around her.

"Augh! Let go! Oh no...!"

The cold grip had found her once more.

Since she had been caught by the white hands, the cold one couldn't lift her—but the boss's piercing attack was clearly imminent. If Maple's HP hit zero again, Indomitable Guardian wouldn't save her.

She immediately called Syrup back out, but her thoughts were too scattered to give it any instructions.

"Um, um! Agh, wh-what now?!"

She was definitely panicking now. And in a race against the clock, all she could do was throw out her default moves, acting on pure instinct and habit.

"Predators! Saturating Chaos! Pandemonium! Hydra! Spirit Cannon! Mother Nature!"

A parade of demons appeared behind her, and two ogres loomed in the darkness above.

A limbless monster appeared on either side of her while another ran out in front, followed closely by the Hydra.

Out in the darkness, thick vines were coiling out of the ground, and with a roar, the Spirit Cannon fired in the direction the Hydra had gone.

The ogres breathed fire, banishing the dark. The air filled with the sound of monster teeth gnashing, clubs pounding, and vines stretching.

"Hnggg!"

The grip holding Maple in place loosened, and she whipped out her collection of charms, frantically slapping them on the hand around her.

Any second now it might end her—for the first time, Maple felt the fear of imminent defeat.

But before her HP vanished—she heard something shatter.

And dazzling light pierced the darkness.

"Wha...?!"

The shroud around her shattered like glass and crumbled away, replaced with light.

When all the dark was gone, she was left in a featureless white room.

"Huh...eh-heh-heh. Thanks, everyone!"

Relieved, Maple flopped over on her back, staring up.

And smiled at the menagerie staring down at her.

"...Right, gotta chug a potion."

She sat up and grabbed a potion from her inventory.

Once her HP was restored, she slowly stood up.

"Whew...that was a close one. But what did the trick? Did instant death kick in, by any chance?"

Maple stretched, looking around.

All that darkness had turned to pure white. Maple couldn't even tell how big the room was.

"Let's see... Yup, over there! Oh, bye-bye, ogres!"

Maple waved, and their time ran out. Her demon army vanished.

Only Syrup and her Predators remained. With them in tow, she headed to her new destination.

"I saw this for an instant on the peak..."

There was a weather-beaten cross stuck in the ground at the center of the white room, with withered flowers all around.

Maple bent down to look, and a voice whispered in her ear.

"Thank you...and good night."

"Wh-who said that?!"

Maple peered up and saw light rising from the cross.

The light took shape, and a woman appeared in front of her.

She extended her hand in Maple's direction—then the light rose skyward, and she was gone.

"...Was it that ghost I fought? Does that mean I exorcised it... or helped it pass on somehow? Hmm?"

She felt something around her neck and touched it.

That was the moment she realized she was wearing a pendant.

"Oh, a locket? There's a picture inside... Could it be that woman? It's so faded I can't really make it out."

From the few surviving details, she could just about see a woman standing in a field of flowers.

Maple took the locket off, checking the description.

"Oh, it's not just any random item; it's an accessory. Helping Hands? Did I help her? I'm not even sure how that fight ended."

Maple had been in such a panic, she had no idea what move had earned her the victory.

She gave up trying to figure it out and decided to read the rest of the accessory description.

Helping Hands

Accessory.

Adds two equipment slots to the hands.

"Wow! That's perfect for Sally. I kinda want one…but I also don't wanna come here again. I'm not even really sure how I got here in the first place."

Maple was already dead set on giving this accessory to Sally.

She quickly sent her a message, asking to meet up on the fifth stratum.

Sally answered soon after, so Maple made her way down a floor.

◆□◆□◆□◆□◆

When Maple reached the fifth-stratum Guild Home, she found Sally waiting for her.

"Hey, Sally! Sorry for the sudden call."

"No prob. What's up?"

"Well, I finally found a way to pay you back for all your help, so…I got eager. Here!"

With that, she took the boots and locket out of her inventory.

Sally instantly realized these must be sixth-stratum gear, and she recoiled, closing her eyes.

After a minute, she managed to open one eye just wide enough to look.

"Mm…hmm. N-not *too* bad. The shoes are a little creepy… There's nothing *in* them, right?"

"Huh? Um, no, I don't think so."

Maple poked the toes, making sure.

Sally carefully took them from her and checked the descriptions.

"These aren't the shoes I was originally after, but…they're actually stronger. And the locket is…wow. That's nuts!"

The ability to equip two extra pieces of gear was absolutely game warping, and Sally gave Maple a look of disbelief. Her head spun with questions, but none of them quite managed to become words.

"It'll be hard to get another one…and I don't really know how I got there. So take care of it!"

"Um…yeah. I will. Thanks!"

Maple's smile was so bright Sally decided that was the only response she needed.

"I'll go try it out!"

"Have fun!"

Maple waved her out the door.

Then she flopped down on the sofa, wriggling with joy over how pleased Sally had been.

Then the next day…

Sally gave the locket back.

"Er, you're sure? It's yours!"

Maple assumed Sally was just feeling guilty, but Sally shook her head.

"Sorry, Maple. I can't use that."

Her voice was a whisper, and question marks appeared over Maple's head.

"Maple…equip that in the field. While you do that, I'm going to stay right here."

With that, Sally fled into the back.

"Hmm…"

Maple decided to do as she was told. She headed out to the field and put the Helping Hands on.

"Yikes?!"

Two transparent hands emerged from behind her, hovering in the air to either side.

"Ah. Okay, yeah... I thought you passed on, ghost!"

The locket's name was *very* literal.

The hands in front of her had nothing past the wrists, and there was no way Sally could tolerate *that*.

"Also, you didn't help Sally at all! More like...argh."

Maple decided that in the future she'd better try things out herself before giving them to Sally.

It might have been a terrible gift, but Maple didn't have a problem using this herself.

She put her gear back the way it had been and opened her stat menu, checked her accessory slots, and thought things over.

Maple

Lv50   HP 40/40 <+160>   MP 12/12 <+10>

[STR 0]   [VIT 250 <+1755>]
[AGI 0]   [DEX 0]
[INT 0]

Equipment

Head	[None]	Body	[Black Rose Armor: Saturating Chaos]
R. Hand	[New Moon: Hydra]	L. Hand	[Night's Facsimile: Devour]
Legs	[Black Rose Armor]	Feet	[Black Rose Armor]
Accessories	[Bonding Bridge] [Toughness Ring] [Life Ring]		

Skills

Shield Attack, Sidestep, Deflect, Meditation, Taunt, Inspire

HP Boost (S), MP Boost (S)

Great Shield Mastery VII, Cover Move VI, Cover, Pierce Guard, Counter

Absolute Defense, Moral Turpitude, Giant Killing, Hydra Eater, Bomb Eater, Sheep Eater, Indomitable Guardian Psychokinesis

Fortress, Martyr's Devotion, Machine God, Quick Change, Bug Urn Curse, Zone Freeze

Pandemonium I, Green's Grace, Heaven's Throne, Nether Nexus

"Hmm, I'll have to take a ring off to equip Helping Hands, but I can't take Bonding Bridge off."

If she did that, she would no longer be able to summon Syrup.

Syrup was her precious partner, so she would definitely have to remove one of the other accessories.

"In that case, I think it'll have to be the Toughness Ring. I'll have thirty less HP, but...I can just raise my defense more instead!"

Maple happily nodded to herself and tucked the Toughness Ring away in her inventory, equipping the Helping Hands instead.

Pale hands appeared in the air, one on either side of her.

And two extra equipment slots appeared on her menu.

"I guess...White Snow and Amethyst Geode? Looks like I can't choose any equipment I have set to Quick Change."

With the extra shields, Maple's VIT was boosted by another

seventy points. And with skills factored in, that number increased sixfold.

Maple looked back and saw each of the Helping Hands holding a shield.

"Oh, looks like I can move them around! It's...really hard..."

If Maple pictured the hands moving in her head, they obeyed.

It was sort of like having two extra arms.

"I found it easy enough to move Atrocity, but this is way...way harder."

She practiced moving the shields around for a while, but either both would move the same way, or she'd focus too hard on one, leaving the other at a standstill. It seemed like it would be a long time before she got the hang of them.

"Well, this is good enough for now!"

She pulled both shields in close and held her own shield up as well.

A veritable wall of shields was arrayed in front of her, and most things would bounce right off.

"I think I'll just practice this for now."

She spent some time pulling the shields into a mini phalanx.

"I need to get better at using my great shield in the first place. Maybe I should ask Chrome."

With that in mind, she headed back to the Guild Home.

Since her extra shields were an accessory, not a skill, they didn't go away even while she was in town.

As a result, a lot of passing players did a double take, stopping dead in their tracks to stare or take photos to report to their guilds.

Maple noticed none of this and cheerily swept into her Guild Home.

She found Chrome relaxing on a couch inside.

"Hey, Mapl— Oh."

Chrome caught up fast and did his best to greet her with a smile.

Maple looked delighted and ran up to him.

"Chrome! I could use some help getting better with shields."

"By that you mean...with these extra floating ones?"

"Exactly! I've got more hands now, but they're hard to use."

"Yeah, not every day you get more...hands..."

Figuring he'd just do what he could to help, he followed Maple back to the training room.

She also showed off Heaven's Throne, which was enough to send Chrome over the edge.

For the heck of it, they tried sparring, and Chrome swiftly came to the conclusion that even if Maple never learned to control the hands with any precision, it wouldn't really matter.

While she was perched upon her throne, the occasional piercing attack would pose no real threat, and with extra shields, the odds of a piercing attack hitting her directly were even lower.

And if she stood up, she could enter Atrocity mode; even sitting down, Indomitable Guardian would save her in a pinch. While she was enthroned and immobile, her party could more than make up for her lack of mobility—it let them focus on attacking, too.

"Yeah, I don't think I'd be able to beat her. Especially not while she's on that throne. That said, it's definitely not all-powerful."

Chrome decided he'd just have to help her compensate for those deficiencies, and he started teaching her what tricks he could think of.

----

641 Name: Anonymous Great Shielder
Sup

*   *   *

642 Name: Anonymous Spear Master
We already know

643 Name: Anonymous Archer
They've multiplied.
Maple, surrounded by shields.
And extra hands!

644 Name: Anonymous Mage
So much extra defense...

645 Name: Anonymous Great Shielder
I sparred with her a bit and came to report in, but...y'all are one step ahead.
I'll lay my take on you anyway.

646 Name: Anonymous Greatsworder
No need to say anything that might undermine her.

647 Name: Anonymous Great Shielder
Gotcha.
First, like you saw, she has extra hands.
All the shields stats and skills are still in effect.
So she's even more impregnable, but given Maple's existing stats, it's honestly a drop in the bucket.

Frankly, the fact that there's even more stuff between you and her now boggles the mind.
And she can *move* them.

*   *   *

How do you hit someone with three shields?

648 Name: Anonymous Archer
That's life and death for an archer.
Also, she can control them all?!
I'm screaming.

649 Name: Anonymous Great Shielder
She's not great at using shields yet, so there's still room to improve.

That's a pretty big *yet*.

650 Name: Anonymous Spear Master
The top great shielder ain't even using her shield...how can you not laugh?

It's like she's still got shackles on.
Part of me is screaming at her to never learn.

651 Name: Anonymous Great Shielder
Oh, *and*
I finally saw the throne firsthand.
It doesn't naturally grow from the turtle shell.

652 Name: Anonymous Mage
We figured.

653 Name: Anonymous Archer
Normally, you just drop it on the ground.

*　　*　　*

654 Name: Anonymous Great Shielder
And when she does, it still generates that white zone when she's
sitting on it.

And the throne blocks some skills.
Several of mine were sealed.
Probably all the crazy skills...
Which probably affects Maple, too.
Dunno the deets.

Oh, and it heals her.

655 Name: Anonymous Greatsworder
That's way too hard a hit to save for a finisher.
If she's sitting there and has *any* friend with her, she's already won.

656 Name: Anonymous Mage
But if it blocks crazy skills...does she have anything left?

657 Name: Anonymous Spear Master
Does it seal Maple herself?

Because she's worse than all her minions.

658 Name: Anonymous Archer
She's *nice* while she's sitting down.
Probably a good idea to not make her stand.

659 Name: Anonymous Greatsworder
She was always a great shielder...

But her protection skills being what they are...
the more friends she has, the stronger she gets.

When she's rolling with the whole guild, ain't no one taking that castle down.

660 Name: Anonymous Spear Master
Her guards too stronk.
When they're in her zone...

Only option is to stealth in and sneak attack.

Maple's the queen now.
Royalty get assassinated all the time.
Might work.

661 Name: Anonymous Great Shielder
I dunno.
Not sure what resists she has besides poison, and can you take her before she's got it all up and running?

662 Name: Anonymous Greatsworder
Maybe a raid boss.

No normal human could do it.
No superhuman could do it, either.
Masters would sense the threat and stay away.
Our only hope is a boss programmed to charge in guns blazin'!

663 Name: Anonymous Mage
But if it can beat Maple in a slugfest, ain't nobody else taking that thing.

*   *   *

664 Name: Anonymous Great Shielder
Anyway, that's all for Maple updates.
I'ma go teach her some more shield skills.

Later!

665 Name: Anonymous Greatsworder
He's gonna make her unstoppable!

666 Name: Anonymous Spear Master
She already is!

667 Name: Anonymous Greatsworder
True. True.

They then spent some time discussing what sort of country Maple would rule, but that's another story.

CHAPTER 7

Defense Build and Helping Out

Maple was getting regular shield-handling lessons from Chrome, but today she was free, which gave her a chance to spend some time on the sixth stratum again.

"Hmm. I've already given Sally her things, so what else should I do?"

She wandered aimlessly for a while but concluded that she didn't really have anything she *had* to do before the next event started.

"I suppose I should just relax! Fighting ghosts is *hard*."

Maple plopped down on a town bench, watching ghostly apparitions fly overhead. Then she received a message.

"Hmm? Who's it from...? Oh, Mii!"

Maple read it over.

It was a basic suggestion that they go hunt monsters together—if Maple had no other plans today, of course.

"I'm definitely not doing anything, so... Okay, looks like we're meeting up at the east exit."

Maple hopped to her feet and headed to their rendezvous.

BOFURI: I DON'T WANT TO GET HURT, SO I'LL MAX OUT MY DEFENSE., VOL. 6

* * *

When she arrived, Mii was already there.

"Sorry! Was I too slow?" Maple asked.

Mii glanced around, making sure no one here knew her.

"Nah," she said. "Thanks for joining on such short notice."

"Oh, I had nothing better to do, so..."

"Yeah? But even so—thanks. Let's get going."

"Sure!"

Maple followed after Mii.

The farther they got from town, the fewer people they saw, and Mii could finally relax.

"You sure I don't need to use Atrocity? I know you can walk faster than me."

"It's fine! I'd rather enjoy the company."

And so they continued their casual stroll, catching up as they walked to their destination.

Along the way, they traded stories from the last event and discussed various enemies they'd fought on the sixth stratum.

Mii wasn't the biggest fan of the town's general vibe. She and Sally had that in common.

They were still talking when they arrived.

"Hmm. That *is* a grave."

"That it is. Supposedly wisps spawn here and you can get a skill that boosts fire attacks. But they use a lot of powerful area attacks."

"I've got you covered! Martyr's Devotion! Heaven's Throne!"

Maple's wings unfurled, her hair turned gold, and her eyes turned crystal blue.

A glittering halo appeared above her head, and a gleaming white throne stood behind her.

96

Maple took a seat and smiled at Mii.

"Whenever you're ready. Oh, just make sure to not get too far away."

"Um. O-okay…got it."

Mii forced herself to stop gaping and focus on the wisps spawning around them.

"Flame Empress!"

Two spheres of fire appeared around Mii, and they started swallowing up the nearby wisps.

But these things seemed to have high elemental resistance—they *did* give a skill that enhanced fire, after all—and even with Mii's flames, one hit was hardly enough.

"That's what I was afraid of. And this is the buffed version!"

Mii waved an arm to attack again—and the swarm of wisps all belched flames as one, blanketing their area in blue fire.

"……! Oh! Right."

Wreathed in those flames, Mii glanced over her shoulder.

Maple was on her throne, bathed in fire, soaking all the damage for her…and still at full HP.

With an impervious fortress protecting her, no mere wisps stood a chance against Mii.

"Wow. I can refill my MP whenever I want!"

Mii downed an MP potion and dived back in, holding nothing back. It did not take long for her infernos to abolish the wisps.

After polishing off a few dozen wisps, Mii joined Maple at her throne.

"Thanks, Maple. Huge help."

"All done? That was amazing! I couldn't see anything but blue fire! It was real pretty."

"That's…nice? I guess? You're about the only person who'll see it from that vantage point."

"Oh? Well, then, I must be lucky!"

"That's one word for it. Hmm…I'd like to thank you somehow… Oh! I know." Mii knocked her palm with a fist. "You're still raising your defense, right?"

"Mm? Oh yeah! I've gotta keep going until I *never* take damage!"

"Ah-ha-ha, I figured as much. In that case, the info broker in town was talking about two related skills. Iron Body and Heavy Body. Something to do with VIT or resistances—the price for the intel was pretty steep, but all they said was they're located 'down south.' I assume that means they're pretty good skills…"

"You can *buy* info on new skills?!"

Maple gaped up at her, but Mii looked every bit as shocked by this response.

"Y-you didn't know that? It isn't cheap, but it can lead you to good stuff."

Mii filled Maple in on the sixth stratum's info broker's location.

"Hngg…there's still so much I don't know! Thanks, Mii."

Maple wrote it all down.

"I should be thanking you!" Mii grinned, stretching. "It sure is nice only having to worry about offense."

"Well, since we're already partied up and everything, wanna go anywhere else?" Maple asked. "Obviously, only if you have time."

"Sure. You turned this into a breeze, so…wanna grab a bite to eat somewhere?"

"Sounds great! Let's get going. I know a good place!"

"Ha-ha, you know more about restaurants than the map, huh?"

"……Maybe."

* * *

Talking about this and that, they returned to the sixth-stratum town. Maple led Mii to a café on the outskirts.

Mii looked around, making sure there were no other players here.

"Looks normal enough," she said. "Good place to relax."

"This stratum has lots of shops that look like ruins, but the insides are all way nicer."

Maple had been relieved to find their Guild Home was the same way.

The two of them took a seat by the window and ordered.

"How'd that last event go for you?"

"Not bad. I was lucky enough to bump into Misery, so we got pretty far. Also we worked with Chrome and Kanade for a while... They're definitely getting strong."

"Heh-heh-heh! Everyone in my guild is great."

"How'd you do?"

"I only made it to the jungle once! The tickets were so hard to find—and I'd rather play with my friends. *Sigh*...I hope they add a new stratum soon so I can play with Sally again."

"I thought I hadn't seen her around—is something up?"

On previous stratums, Mii had regularly caught glimpses of a blue streak destroying all monsters with freakish dodges.

"Um...she's just not a fan of the whole vibe here, so she's skipping this floor."

"Oh...wait, really? Huh. I always thought of her as the kind of person who can handle *anything*."

"She can deal with just about everything except this. She's spent the whole time grinding on floor five. I've helped out some, but..."

"That's nice of you."

"Eh-heh-heh... We're always together outside, too!"

Maple looked pleased as punch. Sally might have strong-armed her into playing, but these days Maple was actually having more fun than Sally.

"You don't go exploring with your guild members, Mii?"

"Ah-ha-ha. No, I definitely do. It's just…easier with you sometimes. But Misery's also on to me, so I can relax around her now, too."

Mii had an image to maintain, and fighting alongside anyone else necessitated a lot of acting. That was making her less than enthusiastic.

"If I'd known it would end up like this, I never would've tried role-playing…"

"Mm-hmm. It does seem exhausting."

"It really takes a lot out of me! I just got these really cool skills early on and thought I'd have a little fun, but now I'm stuck being an empress all the time. I was such an idiot…"

Mii collapsed on the table, rubbing her forehead against it.

At first, it had been fun—the performance had gone hand in hand with her combat style. But things got steadily out of hand, and before she knew it, she was running one of the biggest guilds around.

"Well, feel free to call me anytime you need a break!"

"Mm, I will," Mii said, not even sitting up.

As she spoke, the door swung open—and Maple waved.

"I knew it! Maple and Mii! Yoo-hoo!"

"Frederica and Kasumi? Since when do you two hang out?"

Mii yanked her head off the table, sitting bolt upright.

"Just doing recon. I swung by your Guild Home, but Sally was out again!"

"Ah-ha-ha, she always is."

What Frederica called recon was really just her usual challenging Sally to yet another duel. She insisted she wasn't giving up until she emerged victorious, but Sally always won, and these days, Iz was offering her a cup of tea before she left.

"So I figured I'd blow Kasumi up instead!"

"And I just finished cutting her down."

"...True," Frederica admitted, sitting down next to Kasumi.

"Iz was out today," Kasumi explained. "I've had my fill of exploring, so I thought I'd join her for a breather."

That was when they'd spotted the two of them through the window.

"We were out hunting monsters! Mii was amazing! She burned everything up. The flames were so pretty."

Maple went on at length about the dazzling inferno a few moments longer, eyes sparkling.

"I, too, continue striving to improve," Mii growled. "I've acquired yet more powerful spells and skills."

"Oh...r-right. Almost forgot."

Maple was not very good with subterfuge and was clearly flustered by Mii's abrupt shift in attitude.

Frederica frowned at them for a second but clearly decided it wasn't worth thinking about.

"Cool. We wanna go up against you again sometime, too, Maple! We haven't clashed since the fourth event."

"I won't go down easy! Everyone says I'm getting stronger."

"Well, Pain is, too."

"Not gonna take her on yourself?" Kasumi chuckled.

Frederica made a face. Clearly, she would if she thought she stood a chance.

"If you want to beat Maple, you'll at least need to beat me."

"Teleporting behind me isn't fair!"

"Sally foiled that first try."

"Ugh, that's even less fair."

"Eh-heh-heh! Sally's amazing."

"Next event we get…I dunno when that'll be, but we'll win this time! You feel the same way, right, Mii?"

"Mm? A-ah, indeed. As the Flame Empire guild master, I cannot allow a loss to stand."

The indomitable grin on Mii's face was no performance.

Maple raised a fist high. "Come one, come all! Oh, but if you don't have piercing attacks, that's way better for me."

"We can't win without 'em!" Frederica wailed. "And there's a lot of weirdo Maple sightings lately—I've seen you summon crazy stuff with my own eyes!"

Maple wondered what that meant.

"Wh-which stuff?" she asked.

Quite a lot of her move set seemed to surprise people, and even she could recognize that a few of her recent acquisitions were pretty out there.

"Mm? How much is there?!"

"I imagine even we don't know it all." Kasumi sighed.

"Just standing near Maple makes anyone mad powerful…," Frederica grumbled. She alone could not hope to penetrate Maple's area defense.

"I sit down to fight now! Um, because I have a throne."

"Huh?! Argh. Of course you do."

Frederica looked rather stunned, and Kasumi chuckled.

"I thought I was used to this side of Maple, but when she first showed us the throne, even I couldn't believe it."

Mii nodded emphatically. Clearly, she shared the same opinion.

They all ordered drinks and desserts and chatted for a bit. But Kasumi and Frederica both had things to do, so they didn't stay long.

"I've been looking for a pet monster like your turtle. I was wondering if the sixth stratum had any pet ghosts," Frederica said. She was watching Maple's face awfully closely...and then started looking a bit shifty.

"Hngg, don't you dare use that against Sally!"

"Ha-ha-ha, gave myself away?"

"You better not! Or I'll come bite your head off in the next event!" Maple said, snapping her teeth. She made it sound like a joke, but in a real battle, she'd be in Atrocity form. It would not be nearly as cute then.

"You can actually do that, so...it scared the absolute crap out of me."

"After today, you'll be wanting to duel me again, right? I'm sure we'll see you around often enough. You should take a run at Maple sometime."

"Ugh...no, thanks!"

Frederica more or less ran out, and Kasumi followed, waving good-bye.

Mii and Maple were alone once more.

"...They gone?

"Yup, coast's clear!"

Mii let out a long sigh and slumped back against her chair.

"That was close... I should have known someone might stop in."

"I had no idea how to react when you suddenly got all badass."

"Oof. It's extra mortifying having to act in front of someone who knows the truth..."

Mii mussed up her hair, then took a deep breath, regaining her composure.

"Next time, let's go somewhere more off the beaten track. Sally and I are still checking out previous floors sometimes, so I know a lot of places!"

"See, you're a regular guide. And you're having fun with it, right?"

"It's all places that are new to me, so of course it's fun!"

Maple started listing off places she planned to head next with such obvious delight Mii couldn't help but smile, too.

"That's great. Sounds like a blast. Maybe Misery and I should try a tour like that."

"Yeah! If you spend all your time grinding levels, you'll burn yourself out."

Maple promised to join Mii anytime she asked, happy to have more sightseeing pals.

"Well, if I uncover any more good info, I'll pass it on. You keep an eye out for anywhere I should check out."

"Got it! Will do!"

Once they parted ways, Maple headed south, hoping to stumble upon the skills Mii had mentioned.

CHAPTER 8

Defense Build and Two Girls

Maple made her way south, only occasionally getting tripped up by skeletal hands around her ankles. Eventually she found a house every bit as big as the one she and Sally had visited.

"Hngg, I'd love to check it out, but I can't use Atrocity inside... Should I?"

She waffled a bit, then decided to go in anyway.

"Hello, the house! Gosh, it's huge."

The entrance hall was certainly imposing.

A sweeping staircase led up to the second floor and down to the basement below.

On the far wall was a portrait of a gentleman—worse for wear but still recognizable.

"Hmm. Where should I go first? The basement? Basements seem like the natural place to stash things."

Without a glance at the first-floor doors, Maple headed down the stairs.

"What'll I find...urp?!"

Her enthusiasm was somewhat dashed by spears that shot out of the wall. One did its best to impale her head, eliciting a yelp.

"Wh-what the heck? Whew. You startled me!"

The spear's thrust had stopped the instant it made contact with Maple, not even denting the skin on her brow.

"Oh, the stair is uneven. This must be one of those traps you step on."

Maple wriggled her way past the spears and headed farther in.

At the bottom of the stairs was a long hall with doors on either side.

"Guess I'll just try them all! This could take a while."

Maple took a step forward, headed for the nearest door.

But her foot caught on a taut thread stretched across the hall.

"Mm? Mmm?!"

There was a loud noise overhead, and a guillotine blade dropped—far too fast for her to dodge.

It landed right on top of her head and shattered.

"......? ......??"

Maple rubbed her head, but there was nothing there.

There were bits of broken blade all around, and she bent over, picking one up.

"Was it really fragile? But maybe entering this basement was a mistake. If there's more traps like this, I'm gonna be a nervous wreck."

Maple looked around suspiciously, trying to spot any more traps, but didn't see anything odd.

"Maybe I should head back up...huh?"

Maple turned around but discovered the stairs were gone, replaced with a blank wall.

"Wh-why?!"

Maple banged the wall with her shield, hoping she could break through, but Devour didn't activate. Clearly this wall was indestructible.

"...Oh well! Guess I'll have to explore. Maybe the skills I'm after *are* down here!"

She put the stairs out of her mind—and forgot to watch her step.

There was a clunk underfoot, and the walls closed in.

"Oh no!"

She broke into a run, but before she made it to the end of the hall, she was trapped, pinned between the walls.

"They're crushing meee...or not? But I can't move, so...hnggg."

Maple forced her artillery to deploy and cast Hydra, but the walls simply refused to take damage.

She was stuck with them pressing lightly against her sides for a while, but eventually they started to reset themselves.

"Now what? The floor and the air both have traps everywhere..."

Maple didn't really feel like moving.

Since none of these traps could hurt her, she didn't really have anything to worry about, but Maple hadn't worked that out yet.

"I need a solution...hmm..."

She thought for a minute, then had a brilliant idea.

"Hokay...now if I put this one above me... It worked!"

Maple had one of her Helping Hands great shields lowered to waist height and managed to scramble up, lying down upon it.

Then she had the other shield float on top of her, and she held Night's Facsimile out in front with her actual hands.

She was pinched between two shields like a clam, and Helping Hands was keeping them floating above the ground.

"Cool, it actually worked! Now I won't step on any traps!"

Maple had Helping Hands push her along. Pinned between her shields, she wafted off down the corridor, never touching the ground.

When her eyes caught the gleam of a thread stretched across the hall, it was already too late.

"Ah?! Wai—!"

Too flustered to control Helping Hands properly, she ran right into it, and Devour gobbled the thread up.

More spears popped out, doing absolutely no damage, but Maple was dejected since her clever plan hadn't worked out. Thus—

"Wool Up!"

Wool puffed out all around her and her shields, leaving a giant white ball floating in the air.

"I don't even care anymore! I can't even *hear* the traps going off!"

Safe inside her furball, Maple wafted down the hall.

Several more traps were activated, but she didn't see any of them.

Guillotines, poison arrows, and spears springing from the floor and ceiling were all activated—none of them hurt Maple.

The mansion's traps could no longer even provoke a reaction from her.

"When I hit the wall, I'll make a turn—let's just start from the very back. Good things are always at the back! That's where people hide the best treasures!"

And thus the floating ball of wool triggered and destroyed every trap in the hall.

A while later...

"Oh, I hit a wall! Left... Can't move. Right it is! ...Hngg?"

Bobbing along in her fluffball, Maple had heard far too many traps activate and barely even noticed the clanking noises anymore.

"What's going on...?"

Finding herself unable to go left, right, or backward, Maple poked her head out of the wool.

That was when she realized she was trapped inside a cage made of steel bars.

"Break out!"

Maple shoved her shield forward, smacking the bars.

Devour carved a huge hole, and the cage itself turned to light.

"Whew, that was way less sturdy than I thought. I guess not being able to see has its downsides. I should at least look where I'm going."

Wearing a giant wool mane, Maple started down the hall again.

Sometimes the walls sprayed poison gas, and the floor would open up without warning, but none of it hurt Maple, and she was doing hunky-dory.

"Oh, a dead end. I've come a long way—this *has* to be the end!"

A door stood before her.

Since she'd made up her mind to start at the end, she reached a hand out of the wool, turning the knob.

"Hng…I'm stuck! Rahhh…and I'm in!"

She had to pull pretty hard to squeeze the sphere of wool through the door, but she managed it eventually.

Maple looked around.

Stubby candles lined the walls, along with several well-used suits of armor.

Each of the latter held weapons, and from here, they looked ready for battle.

At the far end of the room was an especially gaudy set of armor. Maple locked her eyes on that.

"Is *that* the boss? I bet it is."

She tried to float closer, but as she neared the center of the room, she noticed a piece of paper lying on the floor.

"Whoa there...lower me a bit..."

She bobbed low enough to reach down and pick up the page.

"Is this note meant for me? Um, let's see. The more traps I triggered the stronger it gets...? Uh-oh!"

As she read that far, a bunch of chains rattled down from the ceiling. In the blink of an eye, Maple was thoroughly bound.

Before she could even react, she found herself and her wool wrapped in chains, unable to move in any direction.

She tried to move the shields with Helping Hands, but her gear was bound securely, and all she could do was rattle the chains.

"Wh-what now?"

As Maple hung suspended, the suits of armor clanked to life—easily twenty in all.

And the gaudy suit was moving, too—far more nimbly than the others, as if a real person was inside.

"T-time out!"

Maple yanked her head back inside the wool, trying to get a grip on things.

"Okay, think... They're attacking, but it's not doing anything. Lemme take another look."

She pushed her way out of the wool again, peering around.

Just as a sword came flying right at her.

It bounced off the wool, came to a stop in midair, and after a moment came flying back at her.

"Huh? I assumed someone threw that. Guess not!"

No use waiting for them to run out of things to throw, then. Maple looked around, wondering what else was going on.

"Hng, where's the fancy armor...?"

She'd kept her eye on it since she walked in the room. It was just standing there, not attacking directly—but a pale light surrounded it.

And the same halo of light hung around the sword and spear currently flying at her.

"I'd better take out that armor first, then! Full Deploy!"

Black columns emerged from the wool.

They were like countless new appendages, each with a gun or cannon attached.

"Commence Assault!"

When her artillery started firing, the floating weapons moved into the path of fire, spinning in place and scattering the incoming rounds.

"That's awesome! Or not. Uh, Hydra!"

This time, the Hydra swallowed up the weapons, inexorably pressing onward, almost making it look like her earlier attacks had been holding.

It hit the gaudy armor head-on and sent it flying, leaving a lake of poison in its wake—which ravaged the other suits.

The floating weapons fell to the ground. Now nothing was attacking Maple at all.

"Oh, and the chains gave way. Is that it? Awesome, don't need the wool anymore."

Maple pulled out an item and set the wool on fire. It soon burned away.

She straightened herself up and landed on the ground.

"Hokay. Let's see what it got me!"

But as Maple took a step toward Lake Hydra, light rose up from the gaudy armor, coalescing in the air.

"What's that?" Maple wondered, not really bracing herself.

The light took shape and changed colors.

When the light faded, a little girl was hovering in the air before her.

She had long silver hair, green eyes, and bright green clothes far too nice for this disheveled room.

The girl looked at Maple and giggled.

Maple quickly put her shield up—and a hand reached out from behind her.

She spun around and found a second girl. She looked identical to the first, but this one wore red.

"Now, now, put those dangerous toys away."

Maple's shield and armor peeled themselves off her, floating away. Then they vanished in a puff of purple light.

"Huh?! H-hey!"

"Let's play a *game*."

The green girl spun in the air. There was a clank, and the gaudy armor stood up again, glowing and hovering in the air.

"It'll be *fun*," the red girl said.

The ground rippled and the walls crumbled, the entire shape of the room changing.

New halls stretched in every direction. There were doors on the ceiling and floors—no trace of the original manor layout was left behind.

""Count to ten, then come find us!""

Both girls giggled. One changed into a blue light while the other became purple, and then they both vanished through the walls.

Before Maple could even parse what was happening, the two girls were gone.

"Huh? What? Whyyy?"

She looked around and spotted several suits of armor marching toward her in lockstep.

"Augh! Uh, can't use Hydra or Atrocity…Full Deploy!"

Losing her equipment deprived her of her best weapons, but Maple realized she could still use Machine God if she paid the penalty.

Her body was soon covered in gears and tubes, weapons sprouting everywhere.

"Cool!"

"Oh no you don't! Those are dangerous toys!"

"Dangerous!"

The girls' voices echoed through the room again.

Blue and purple lights swirled around Maple, and all her weapons crumbled away.

"You're kidding!"

"And naughty girls…"

"…need to be punished!"

Spears and swords wreathed in blue light started coming out of the floors and ceiling.

These weapons shot toward Maple.

"Eep!"

She raised her arms, covering her face, and the swords and spears hit home—

"Urp…oh, good. Nothing happened."

Swords, spears, and blows from the suits of armor were all bouncing off her, even without her gear's stats.

Each hit stopped the moment it hit her skin, doing absolutely nothing to her.

"Um, did I have any skills I could use without gear? Oh, Heaven's Throne!"

A white throne appeared behind her.

She gingerly took a seat, worried it would vanish, too, but the girls didn't say a word.

"I see. This isn't considered dangerous. Hmm. So I can't use skills with powerful attacks..."

Pandemonium would probably not work, either. Maple decided to keep that in reserve.

Almost all her big moves were out of commission, and that was the only thing she could fall back on.

Clutching a faint hope that she'd be able to use it if a proper boss fight started, Maple decided to move on, knocking the swords and spears out of the way with her bare hands.

"Urp...way too many doors. And these suits of armor literally won't leave me alone!"

Surrounded by ten suits of armor, their swords slashing away (leaving her unharmed), Maple made it to a door in the wall.

"Ha! Coming through!"

She yanked the door open and jumped through, quickly closing it behind her, both hands braced against it.

But the armor didn't try to follow her through. She breathed a sigh of relief and slumped to the ground.

"Good...but now what? I *do* have another set of equipment, but I don't want them stealing that, too."

Even without her gear boosting her defense and HP, she already had more than enough damage resistance.

The only blows strong enough to penetrate her four-figure VIT would instakill anyone else, and enemies on that scale weren't found just anywhere.

So Maple didn't need to worry about incoming attacks.

"Okay, first things first! Let's go get my equipment back!"

Fired up, she set out down the hall.

She had no idea where the girls were hiding, so she couldn't just breeze on by this time.

There was no choice but to open every door she passed.

Well aware the vast majority would activate traps.

"*Sigh*...hello?"

She took a deep breath and stepped inside, cringing as she looked around.

There was a long table with a cloth on it, chairs neatly lined up, and a single candlestick at the center.

The walls were warped but decorated with paintings of landscapes.

"Um...okay. Other than the twisty walls, nothing weird here."

Maple carefully checked under the table and behind the paintings, but she found nothing.

"I think it's safe... Oh."

She turned back from the last painting to find all the chairs and paintings and the candlestick glowing blue.

"Uh...?! Don't—!"

But her protests were in vain, and the chairs flew at Maple.

"Swords weren't a real problem, but...still! This is too much stuff!"

There was a series of clunks—and Maple was trapped behind a heap of chairs and paintings.

Just as she started clambering over it, a lit candle flew her way.

"Eep?!"

Before she could run, the entire pile went up like a bonfire, leaving Maple trapped in the center.

Ten chairs and a dozen paintings made for a pillar of fire that raged higher than Maple was tall.

When the fire finally burned itself out, Maple was still standing.

"Whew... If you've got nothing else on, your default clothes don't burn! That's nice. But it's still bad for the heart!"

Maple brushed the soot off herself and headed for the door.

The candle was back on the table, and she gave it a baleful glare in passing.

"I think you're far naughtier than I am," Maple said.

She took some glue out of her inventory, rubbed it on the bottom of the candlestick, and put it back.

This was a powerful adhesive that had dropped from a monster she'd fought, so Maple was fairly certain that candle wasn't going anywhere.

"And that's *your* punishment!"

She slammed the door open far harder than she had on the way in.

◆□◆□◆□◆□◆

A good two hours had passed since Maple was first set on fire.

She was moving down the hall, breathing hard.

There was dust, soot, and other dirt all over her.

"Ugh…please no more pitfalls…"

She couldn't use her floating furball anymore, so she'd spent the last hours getting caught by every trap in creation. Set on fire multiple times, dropped into pits repeatedly, assaulted by random suits of armor—she no longer even flinched when guillotine blades or spears shot her way.

And the pitfalls were *definitely* the worst.

They were usually lined with spikes, which didn't do anything to Maple—in fact, they frequently snapped when she fell. But the holes themselves were a huge hassle.

On more than one occasion, she was forced to stab broken spikes into the crumbling walls, making herself incredibly tenuous footholds that tended to drop her back down whenever they failed to hold her weight, so climbing back out of them was *hard work*.

It was so bad it only took two before the light in her eyes went out.

"Sally would probably know exactly how to spot all the traps... but I just can't tell!"

She gingerly took another step...and there was a clunk. The floor sank.

"Eeek!"

She tried to leap away, but something came flying at her.

"......Mm, oh, thank goodness. It's just a poison arrow..."

There was purple liquid slathered on the tip. Maple scooped it up.

No one else would be *relieved* by poison arrows, but Maple's list of priorities was currently dominated by pitfalls—nothing else really mattered at the moment.

"Hmm...I'm pretty far in now... At least, I hope I am."

The walls and hallways were very winding, and sometimes there were doors in the ceiling, so Maple found it hard to judge her progress.

"Let's go this way!"

As always, she let her instincts guide her, opening a door and heading through.

Even without gear, her body repelled all harm, so Maple could move freely through a hundred traps at once.

Despite her sluggish pace, she was still getting through this labyrinth far faster than the average player could have managed.

Maybe half an hour later...

"Oh! That door looks promising."

Maple was squinting down the hall at a particularly conspicuous door.

She'd played this game enough to know what boss rooms looked like.

"Awesome! Time to get my gear back."

She broke into a run, barreling down the hall.

This naturally triggered some traps, but Maple had seen more than her fair share of flying spears and arrows—she didn't even bat an eye.

"I don't care! Just you wait, ghost twins! Heh-heh! I'm gonna make you pay!"

But just as her motivation peaked—the floor beneath her feet split open.

"Urp?! Aughhh!"

The burst of excitement had made her forget all about the danger of pitfalls. She just barely managed to get her fingers on the far ledge, dangling from them—but they were already quivering.

She didn't have the strength to pull herself up.

"Urgh...I'm gonna fall in!"

She glanced down and saw the bottom of the pit filled with green glittering goo.

The blood drained from her face.

She wasn't scared of goo. She was scared that without spikes, she'd have no way of getting out.

"Help! Somebody—aiiiieee!"

Even as she begged for mercy, her fingers gave way, and Maple went plummeting into the depths.

There was a splash as she landed back-first on the goo, and she stared dismally up at the ceiling.

"Ugh...what now? This sure looks poisonous, but that's not a problem. Ew, it's all sticky."

The green goo was a bit chilly but otherwise ineffective.

The problem here was how to get back out.

"I don't wanna log out without getting my stuff back... There's got to be a way out."

Maple closed her eyes, racking her brain.

After she thought very hard, one idea did come to mind.

"Hmm…I know! Full Deploy!"

Weapons bristled…and vanished.

But Maple was not disappointed—she was *delighted*.

"Great! Come on, punish me! I'm right here!"

But the swords or spears she'd been hoping for did not come flying her way.

"Wh-whyyyyyy?! Please? I need you to punish me!"

Her plan had been to stab the wall with those and climb out. Foiled!

Outside the boss room, the players were expected to *avoid* traps.

And since she had charged in without thinking, she found herself well and truly stuck.

"What now…? If only I could make a *lot* of thrones…"

But as Maple slumped, the goo began to *move*.

Before she knew it, she was covered in green.

"Oh, is this a slime? That chill is nice and refreshing. I think I'm feeling a little better."

The slime was wrapping itself tightly around her, trying to dissolve her flesh.

"…Oh! Thank you, slime!"

Having calmed down enough to think, Maple took a deep breath—and spoke the name of a skill.

A short while after Maple fell in the pit, the doors of the boss room swung open.

"Oh, she's here! She's here! She found us!"

"She did! She found us!"

The little twins giggled. All manner of twisted things floated in the air around them.

"Whew…I'm here for my equipment!"

Maple stood inside a green, bubbling sphere.

"I can make things float, too!"

Psychokinesis could make monsters float. It had not *originally* been intended to make Syrup fly. Maple was now using it to alter the slime's shape, giving herself a sword and shield to fight the twins with.

""Heh-heh-heh… Let's begin!""

Swords and spears appeared behind the twins, rocketing toward Maple.

She tried to bob away, but she moved far too slowly to dodge them all.

Weapon after weapon stabbed the slime, but the slime's HP didn't change—and soon the improvised missiles started to dissolve.

"Oh! This slime is amazing! Next…"

Maple used Psychokinesis again, changing its shape. Instead of floating with her inside it, it now formed armor covering her body and provided her with two big slime arms. She'd gotten used to flying Syrup around and had practiced enough with Helping Hands that she could easily pull off this level of telepathic control.

"Mm, this is pretty easy to use! Now…"

The slime arms reached out and grabbed at one of the twins— the green one.

"Aw, they pass right through her. I was hoping a slime would work."

But slime bodies counted as physical attacks, so she couldn't actually hit them.

And their counterattack came from the red girl—in the form of flames.

"Augh! You're weak against fire?!"

The slime's HP had dropped hard, and Maple quickly pulled the arm back.

Once the slime was safely coiled around her again, she looked around the room, trying to find something she could use.

The boss room was decorated like a nursery.

It was pretty big but had desks, closets, furnishings, stuffed animals, toys—more like a place to play than a place to fight.

"There's lots of presents here, but are any of them useful?"

She peered down at her slime. It was still dissolving all the swords and spears.

"Whoops, here comes more fire! I'll take that!"

Before the incoming flames hit, Maple sent the slime away, brushing the flames aside with her bare arm.

The scattered flames lit up a nearby gift box.

"Ack! That's not good."

Maple's slime was weak to fire, and she did *not* want the whole stage turning into a conflagration. She patted the flames with her bare hand, putting them out, and breathed a sigh of relief.

And her hand hit something inside the box—something that hadn't burned.

"Oh! My short sword!"

Maple had discovered her own stolen equipment.

Realizing this, the twin ghosts called out.

"Aw, what now?"

"I don't want it! She can have it."

Sounded like she was free to take it back.

"In that case…Hydra!"

And free to make use of the skill on it.

A three-headed dragon raced off toward the spectral twins.

But they both disappeared, teleporting across the room and neatly dodging the poison.

""Ah-ha-ha! Too easy!""

"Hngg. Then how about…Full Deploy!"

This was the boss room, and Maple was sure all her skills worked again. She started opening fire—

But the twins' projectiles came fast enough that none of hers got through the fusillade.

"We already *saw* that!"

"Yeah!"

They glanced at each other, giggling.

Maple looked rather cross, but she changed up her strategy.

"Well, my other gear must be in these other boxes. I'd better start by finding it. Slime, you hide in the corner."

With the slime out of harm's way, she let spears and swords alike bounce off her back, opening present after present. Even without the slime dissolving them, none of these weapons could hurt Maple.

By the time she finally found all her stuff, the floor was covered in fallen swords, and the walls were riddled with axes and spears.

"Whew… That was exhausting! But this should make the fight easier."

All her gear was back in place. It was time to punish these naughty ghosts.

While she'd been looking, Maple had come up with a plan.

"When you're fighting foes that like to run away—make sure they've got nowhere to go!"

Maple mustered her most diabolical smirk and moved to the exact center of the room.

"Martyr's Devotion! Venom Capsule!"

An angel appeared—but her glittering wings were soon buried in a mass of poison.

A purple sphere looming at the heart of the boss room.

"Predators!"

Maple sat back inside her toxic orb, flanked by monsters.

"Slime, you come over here, too!"

It bobbed her way, and the three monsters took care of all incoming projectiles.

While Venom Capsule was still small, there was a chance it might get splattered by some stray poison—but this strategy kept it safe.

"If fake Sally couldn't get away, I know you can't!"

Maple's goal was to fill the whole room with poison.

These ghosts might be able to teleport all over the shop, but that didn't do much good if the entire room was a death trap.

"Heh-heh-heh," Maple chuckled, moving her slime around. "It might take a while, but I am *very* persistent."

Several hours had passed since Maple started filling the chamber with venom.

Her Predators and slime had kept the capsule safe, and it grew steadily, getting bigger than ever before. Their task done, she put her monsters away—in that sense, everything had gone according to Maple's plan.

She was indeed persistent, and nearly the entire room was filled with poison. But the results were not exactly what she'd hoped for.

"Wait, are they immune to poison...?"

The twins were drenched in it, but they were still flinging weapons and fire around with the same amount of energy as before.

Maple scowled at them awhile, but the poison didn't even seem to be slowing them down.

But as time went on, the target of their attacks had shifted from Maple herself to the slime.

For better or worse, the slime was also immune to poison, and it had stayed alive. It was still under Maple's control, of course.

And it had destroyed so many of the twins' weapons that their aggro was entirely focused on the monster now.

Yet none of their attacks could reach it because of all the toxic goo in the way.

And at this size, Venom Capsule's endurance was far higher than their weak attacks could handle.

Maple once again found herself in a situation where they couldn't beat her, but she couldn't beat them.

"Uh, what next? They just dodge all my attacks... Maybe I could hit them if I was *very* close?"

Figuring it couldn't hurt to try, she foraged through the poison, swimming higher.

Since the entire room was full of goo, she could move freely through it.

"Let's try a few things and see if I can stop them running!"

She started pulling charms out of her inventory, scattering them throughout the venom.

"Hopefully these exorcism charms will stop them from tele-porting...but I'm not banking on it."

Maple scattered any items she didn't think she would need, fill-ing the venom with obstacles, and then she had the slime stretch itself as far as it could, wrapping itself around the twins several times over.

"Okay! Let's try this!"

She had the slime open a hole in the enclosure and reached in.

Maple put the tip of her short sword an inch from one of the girl's bellies.

"Please hit! Hydra!"

Brimming with hope, she unleashed a toxic torrent upon a room that was already brimming with poison.

Naturally, this caused a whirlpool around her.

When her eyes stopped spinning, she looked around to see if it had worked.

"I think they got away? But where— Oh, there they are!"

Maple found them trapped inside the slime (itself barely clinging to life), covered in the items she'd scattered—and immobilized.

"Hmm. Hngg?"

Even Maple could tell this was an unusual state of affairs. Clearly not a typical means of catching them.

"A-are you okay?" she asked, reaching out and poking one of their feet.

"Aw, you caught us!" one said.

"You caught us both!"

""The game's all over!""

Light appeared all around them, concentrating and growing ever brighter.

""Let's play again someday!""

And with that, both twins vanished.

Maple looked around, very confused.

"Oh! They never had HP bars. So I didn't actually beat them?"

Like the snails from an earlier event, the twins had been a foe you had to get past without fighting.

Maple had been too mad about the traps to work that out.

"Still..."

They'd left a treasure chest behind. She swam down to it.

Then she canceled Venom Capsule. Items and low-ranking materials rained down around her.

"I feel like that wasn't what was supposed to happen… I-I'd better get out of here."

Maple ditched the items and materials, shoved the chest in her inventory without looking inside, and promptly ran away.

◆□◆□◆□◆□◆

Behind the scenes…

The devs were frantically trying to fix things.

"It's Maple again! She's basically a walking bug, but we can't have her glitching the game!"

"They're stuck *inside* a slime?!"

"This is all that slime's fault! Who put that thing inside a random trap?!"

"Even if they can't be attacked, if they can't pass through it, the twins'll get stuck!"

"If it weren't for that thing, they could have squished the capsule!"

"Deep breaths! First, adjust the twins' warp parameters. The slime itself is fine! It does its part as a trap, and nobody but Maple could do that with it."

"And she made off with the good stuff *again*."

This was the gear Maple had taken with her. Naturally, they knew what was in the chest.

"But at this point, what difference does it make?"

"…No, this one's pretty bad."

A grim silence settled over the room.

"…True."

With the initial uproar fading, it was all too obvious what horrors their greatest threat would wreak with what she'd just obtained. At the very least, this wouldn't diminish her.

"I swear I'm getting an ulcer."

"Still! It won't up her DPS! Not...directly..."

"But indirectly?"

"It might."

"Then don't get my hopes up. Sure, fine, the other players are all getting stronger, too. If we fix the bug here, it's not that bad. Just...double-check for weird synergies and...pray."

"Only thing we can do."

All heads nodded.

Eventually, there was a short server downtime, and the patch notes mentioned changes to slime behavior in dungeons and the handling of boss monsters getting stuck inside other monsters. Since other monsters rarely spawned in boss rooms, most players had no idea how that would ever be possible.

◆□◆□◆□◆□◆

A while before that happened, Maple came bursting out of the haunted house and briskly walked away, glancing over her shoulder a few times.

"And they didn't even have the skill I wanted!"

Mii had told her about Iron Body and Heavy Body, so she'd been searching for those, but they clearly weren't in this building.

"But I did get something! Uh, where'd I put it...? Oh, there it is!"

Maple took out the chest to find out what was inside.

When she opened the lid, she found green clothes, just like those the one girl had worn.

"Ghost Girl Garb? Hmm. Equipment...oh, but it *does* have a skill."

Maple went ahead and read the skill description, too.

Ghost Girl Garb

[MP+30]

Poltergeist

For 10MP, this spell allows you to move certain objects.
You can control a maximum of ten objects.
Effect lasts five minutes.
But is limited to objects you own.

"My MP's pretty low, so I can't make much use of that skill. But I like the clothes!"

Maple swapped some gear to equip the Ghost Girl Garb.

She was now surrounded by green frills and ribbons.

Maple took one look at it, then summoned Syrup, having it float by her head.

"Eh-heh-heh! We match!"

She smiled at the turtle.

The dress might not be functionally a great match for Maple, but she loved it anyway.

"I can keep *one*."

Maple decided she was going to keep this—as opposed to giving it to Sally.

"Hmm. Better take my shield off...then... Oh, there it is!"

Maple took Helping Hands off, too, replacing it with a little silver crown.

She'd found this with Pain in the jungle—it gave her a 10 percent MP recovery boost.

"They look good together! If I think of a way to fight like this, my gear can have a Syrup colorway!"

Maple began thinking about combat applications.

With most of her gear gone, she was just a normal girl—but still way tankier than anybody else. Her offensive approach might change, but she was otherwise just Maple.

"Hmm. If I'm fighting *with* Syrup...then...hmm..."

At first, she was at a loss, but eventually she reread the Poltergeist description and had an idea.

"I wonder if I can control Hydra?"

She gave it a shot, activated Poltergeist—and found herself with a mass of poison suspended in the air, surrounded by a blue glow.

"Ooo! Then if I want to move it, I can just..."

Maple waved a hand down, and Hydra accelerated, crashing into the pavement and bursting.

"Wow!" Maple yelped, leaping backward. "This seems pretty tricky to use..."

She thought a few minutes longer, but she only had a few Hydra uses remaining, so she tried a different weapon instead.

"Lemme practice a bit."

The results of this practice suggested that at the moment, she could only manipulate two things at once. The description had said the max was ten, but it would be a long time before she could pull that off.

"It's easy to move things if I'm waving my hands around, but... hmm, I'll just have to practice more when I have time."

Maple made Syrup giant, climbed up on top, and went back to practicing. With more ranged manipulation skills, Maple had new things to busy her mind with, and it was urgent that she get used to it.

Manually controlling the flight path of a single bullet to hit a monster in the distance did not really do enough damage to justify the cost and effort.

Maple downed an MP potion and kept experimenting, finding ways to improve and getting better with the skill.

Maple was practicing at the edge of the field but not so far out that no one passed by.

Chrome and Kasumi just happened to be in the area.

Sally, Mai, and Yui were all skipping this floor, so they had limited party options.

"Oh, is that Maple?" Kasumi asked, using her hand as a visor.

"Gotta be. Turtle, weapons sprouting from her back…"

Nobody else in *NWO* matched that description.

They headed her way, planning to say hi—and two bluish lasers shot out of the weapons on her back.

This alone they'd seen before—but instead of vanishing, these lasers stayed put.

And started swinging around like swords.

""……………""

They stopped dead in their tracks, glancing at each other.

"Should we ask? You coming, Kasumi?"

"I'd better. Lord knows what it means."

They were already resigned to learning yet another shocking revelation. Both took deep breaths and approached.

◆□◆□◆□◆□◆

As they got closer, Maple saw them coming. She stopped manipulating lasers and waved.

"Maple, you've got new gear," Chrome said.

"I do! What do you think?!" Maple stood up on Syrup's back and did a little turn.

That alone seemed to make her happy. Before they could even ask, she started babbling about how her outfit was the same color as Syrup and how she'd figured out a good use for the skill.

"By skill you mean…those?" Kasumi pointed at the two lasers above them.

"Yup! It's kinda tricky, but if I… Augh!"

Just as she tried to show them off, the lasers ripped skyward. The skill had timed out after five minutes had passed, and she'd lost control.

"Oof…I've gotta get used to that time limit."

"Well, glad to see you branching out."

"But what'll you do on the equipment front?" Kasumi asked. "You've already got two sets in regular rotation."

Maple grinned, way ahead of her. "Syrup, wait here."

She hopped off and walked a few steps away.

Kasumi was about to ask why when the number of weapons on Maple's back doubled.

She'd seen this before—this was how Maple brute-forced flight.

An instant later, she rocketed skyward, belching flames that trailed behind her. Whatever Maple was doing up there was completely obscured by the smoke and fire.

"What now?"

"You're asking me?"

But even as they exchanged looks, there was a boom, and dust billowed everywhere.

"Wha...?!"

"Yo...?"

When the dust cleared, Maple got to her feet—back in her black gear.

Maple's idea? When she didn't have time to change on the ground, she could just temporarily fly away.

It was safe to say there were no attacks capable of taking Maple out mid-flight. She could temporarily remove all gear without anything hitting her.

Maple dusted herself off and nodded as if at a job well done.

"I can use that in most fights!"

"Yup. I reckon you can."

"Same."

"I'll have to go show Sally!"

They'd need to account for it in future strategy sessions, so there was a function to her showing off her new gear.

Maple put Syrup back in her ring, said good-bye, and headed to the fifth stratum.

As they watched her go, Kasumi muttered, "Well, at least she's on *our* side."

"Yup. And the lasers aren't insanely strong, not like Hydra...but I guess if they stick around for five whole minutes, they're pretty dang OP."

What she'd revealed about this new skill echoed through their minds awhile, but they concluded that *all* Maple's projectiles were ridiculous, and no matter which ones she used, anyone standing on the receiving end was in for a bad time.

◆□◆□◆□◆□◆

Maple reached the fifth stratum and sent Sally a message. The answer came quickly.

"Oh, she's in the Guild Home! Nice!"

Maple trotted off to meet her. When she stepped inside, Sally looked up in surprise.

"Maple— Oh, I see. You wanted to show that off?"

This explained the urgent meeting request.

"Exactly! Doesn't it look great?"

"It does. You've been stuck in armor here, so this is a nice change of pace. And the crown really sells the princess look."

"Ah-ha-ha! I don't think anyone would mistake me for a princess."

"Fair. At least, you'd be the type that makes all the ministers fret."

"Oh? I would?"

The next several minutes were frittered away on idle chatter, but eventually Maple remembered that this gear had *function*.

"Oh, also this gear is good in combat!" she said, and she explained.

Sally nodded. "Sounds good, yeah. Maybe I should take another run at the sixth stratum…"

"Oh?"

Vivid memories flooded Maple's mind.

She gave Sally a long, skeptical look.

"I mean…*some* places might be okay? But, well…"

Sally got very shifty, well aware of how doomed this plan was. She soon abandoned the idea.

"I'll just have to hit the seventh stratum extra hard!"

"Yep! I wanna play with you again. Can't wait till they add it!"

But they would have to wait a little longer before the promised day came.

For now, they kicked back, talking about all the sights they'd seen.

CHAPTER 9

Defense Build and the Seventh Event

A few days after Maple explored the trap-infested manor, she still hadn't managed to achieve her original goal—the acquisition of Iron Body and Heavy Body.

She was now perched on a chair in her Guild Home, legs swinging, lost in thought.

"Hngg...where could they be? They must be out there somewhere... Is this one of those specific-time-of-day things?"

But as her mind wandered further into the woods, her chain of thoughts was interrupted by the bleat of a notification.

"Hmm? Oh! The next event. Um...this time we're clearing dungeons?"

Maple read the announcement over.

This event involved clearing a tower that contained ten relatively small floors. The number of medals awarded depended on the difficulty you selected.

Time was not sped up, but you could teleport to the highest floor you'd cleared—there was no need to complete the entire tower in one run. The event itself was active for a relatively long time, so you just had to pace yourself to finish before it was over.

"Should we all team up and hit the highest difficulty? Oh, but if you clear it solo, you get better rewards."

Clearing the top difficulty in a party would net each participant five medals. But anyone who succeeded solo would get ten.

"But there's no fighting other players this time, good."

That meant Maple could relax and enjoy herself.

The event would start at the beginning of April.

Maple's eyes locked on that date—and she gasped.

"Gosh! It's been a whole year! I almost never stick with *anything* this long."

Maple thought back on all she'd done, and every memory was delightful. Just reminiscing put a smile on her face—even thinking about those scant few tough battles, all the more memorable for the challenges they'd posed.

And that motivated her to go out exploring once more.

"Right, then! Let's get these skills before the next event begins!"

Maple hopped down from her chair and headed out to paint the sixth stratum red.

◆□◆□◆□◆□◆

But her enthusiasm did not improve her outlook.

Maple still had no clue where these skills could be.

"What now...? Oh! I haven't checked the boards in a while."

Feeling proud of herself for even thinking of that, she headed toward the center of town.

Maple wormed her way through the crowd to the boards and found info on both skills so fast she felt like an idiot for worrying about it so long.

"Oh, oh, oh. Looks like they only *just* figured it out! Lessee…"

She read over the intel.

But the descriptions filled her with dismay.

Neither skill was purely VIT based. Both involved MP and STR.

Iron Body

Doubles fire and lightning damage but reduces non-magic damage by 30%.

MP cost: 50. Effect lasts two minutes.

Five-minute cooldown.

Prereq: MP: 50, VIT: 80

Heavy Body

Prevents knockback.

If STR is lower than VIT, you can't move.

MP cost: 10. Effect lasts one minute.

Three-minute cooldown.

Maple couldn't even acquire the first one, and neither seemed particularly good.

She barely took damage to begin with, so reducing it did not seem worth the MP.

And the latter skill would simply leave her stuck in place for a full minute, which seemed irredeemably bad.

"But where do you get them…? Oh! Well, might as well write it down. Hmm, well, I at least meet the requirements for the second one…but is it worth it?"

Maple just didn't really see herself making much use of Heavy Body.

She left the board behind, wandering down the main road, trying to make up her mind.

"It wouldn't *hurt* to have it...and I spent all this time trying to figure it out...so let's at least pick up Heavy Body. First..."

Maple sent a message to several Maple Tree members and headed out to the field to find Heavy Body.

With proper info, she had no trouble felling the monsters in her path.

And it did not take her long to learn the skill.

◆□◆□◆□◆□◆

Time passed. Maple raised her levels a bit and smashed her black armor a few times.

Once again, she'd logged in and arrived at her Guild Home.

The one on the fifth stratum.

Sally was already waiting for her.

"Oh, Maple! The event starts today! What are you thinking? Solo run? All eight of us?"

There was no one else with Maple, so Sally figured the former.

"Neither!" Maple said.

"......?"

"I wanna run this event with you, Sally."

The message she'd sent the other guild members?

It had said she wanted to pair up with Sally this time.

And nobody in Maple Tree was going to argue with that.

"It's been too long since we played together."

Sally looked rather surprised, but then she smiled.

"I like it! In which case…"

"Let's try and win without taking damage!"

"I've been honing my dodge skills on the fifth stratum. They're still alive and well!"

"And I'm fully set to keep you safe!"

With that settled, they headed for the event tower.

Both of them looked ready to dance.

CHAPTER 10

Defense Build and the Tower's First Floor

Maple and Sally arrived at the magic circle in the center of town.

This would take them directly to the event tower.

"We good with the hardest difficulty?"

"Ab-so-lutely! I'm all fired up!" Maple cried.

Sally looked pretty excited herself. "Ha-ha! Then this way. Let's get the first floor cleared!"

"Woo!"

Sally looked confident, and Maple was just having fun.

They stepped on the circle to the hardest tower and vanished in a puff of white light.

When the light faded, they found themselves before a tower so tall it seemed to pierce the heavens.

The top was hidden in the clouds, and the size of each floor was considerable.

"This…is gonna take a while."

"You can say that again. If it's as big as they look, each floor is like a quarter the size of a normal field…but who knows, maybe there are teleport points here and there."

"Rad! Nice and meaty!"

"True. Let's get clearing!"

They headed straight through the doors and into the tower interior.

The hall inside was wide enough for four to walk abreast, and from here they could already see several forks.

The ceiling was a good thirteen feet above them.

"So..."

"Yup, gonna be a real maze. Gotta watch out for ambushes!"

"Oh, well...Martyr's Devotion!"

This was just Maple's default opening move in situations like this. Her angelic protection would keep Sally safe if anything went wrong.

Angel wings rose up from the back of her black armor.

Once they were ready, they set off through the dungeon.

"Oh, right, Maple...you aren't using the extra-shields thing?"

"I'm still working on that. Feels like it'll be a while before I can move multiple things at once. Besides, it would bother you, right?"

"Urp...yeah, a bit. An eensy-teensy bit."

Sally's feelings aside, Maple had a lot of moving-things-with-her-mind skills she needed to practice. She'd decided to put a pin in all that for now.

If she needed to, she could always just change up her equipment piecemeal.

Maple was getting good at buying herself that kind of time.

Sally, on the other hand, thought Helping Hands was good enough that she should really try and learn to look directly at it without freaking out.

"Will I ever manage...? Oops! Maple, look out!"

Mid-thought, she spotted something ahead.

"Huh? Oh…"

Maple had been too focused on their conversation and had completely missed the telltale sign of the floor changing color. She'd stepped right onto it.

The floor yawned open, and Maple fell straight down.

Sally shot her webs at the wall and didn't go anywhere.

"Maple, you okay?"

"Yeah! It's just poison." Maple's voice echoed from the pit below.

Not long after, Maple rose up from the depths, pinned between two shields held by ghastly hands.

"Ha-ha! If I've got the right gear, pitfalls ain't no thing!"

"…I'm glad you're okay, b-but let's try to watch our step."

Sally was squinting so she wouldn't see the Helping Hands too clearly. She wasn't even looking in Maple's direction.

"…Oh, I know! Wool Up!"

What had led Maple to transform into a ball of fluff? From which emerged her face and a pair of angelic wings?!

"Maple…"

"Now I don't have to care about traps! And you won't be scared! The perfect solution! I ran a whole dungeon like this before."

Maple bobbed over to Sally and helped her inside.

"Forwaaard!"

"O-okay? Does this even count as running a dungeon?"

While Sally pondered the semantics, Maple started them drifting down the hall.

"Um, Maple. Monsters ahead."

A bird came flapping around the corner. It was a yard long, with red wings.

"Mwa-ha-ha! Doesn't matter which way you come! Full Deploy! Commence Assault!"

Black pillars rose up from the sea of wool, deploying guns and cannons.

Maple started pouring fire into them with great confidence, but all the attacks went right through the bird's body. The bird itself turned into pure fire before immediately dive-bombing them.

"Maple!"

"Ack! Er, um...anything but that!"

Unfortunately, the floating furball was not exactly mobile, and the bird's swoop burned all the wool away.

"Hmph!"

"We gotta fight! Back me up!"

"Got it! Then...Taunt!"

Maple hopped off her floating shield and used a skill to keep the firebird on her.

Trying to keep Devour in stock, she let it hit her head-on while Sally slung water spells from the side.

That magic caused it to spray red damage sparks, and its flames diminished—it was now just a regular red-winged bird again.

"Yup, I thought fire would be weak to water."

Sally drew her daggers and piled on more damage.

"Maple!" she called.

"It's payback time...Hydra!"

A purple torrent swallowed the bird.

And the Bug Urn Curse instakill kicked in. The bird vanished without a trace.

Both girls took the opportunity to catch their breath.

"Lemme just take Helping Hands off... Whew."

"Hmm, nice work. That was basically a normal mob with a twist on top, but glad we got through it."

"But now I can't Wool Up..."

"Can't rely on your old exploits. You gotta learn to spot the traps!"

"Yeah, I guess. I'll just have to try harder!"

Maple triggered several more traps, but they made steady progress despite that.

They went right and left. Several fights in, they were definitely seeing why this dungeon was the highest difficulty.

"These things suck."

"Yeah…they're all bad news."

Neither one of them was fazed by mere strength, but the monsters were all immune to physical damage, or they were immune to magical damage, or it was only possible to defeat them if you met a specific condition—every trick in the book.

Sally's Sword Dance had hit max stack in a single fight with a monster that kept bounding around the walls.

The devs had clearly designed these foes to give top-tier players like Maple a run for their money.

And yet another new monster appeared before them. Like a cloud that had taken human form.

"Sally, another weird one!"

"Maybe it's a variant on the fifth-stratum enemies? Careful!"

Maple still had Martyr's Devotion up, and she was also walking in front of Sally, shield at the ready.

Sally lurked behind her, waiting for her chance to strike.

The cloud monster spotted them and got ready to fight.

There was a momentary pause, then a green glow charged up inside its body, filling the passages with blades of wind.

"Maple!"

"Mm!"

Their previous battles had left her with seven Devour uses, and she wanted to save those—so she lowered her shield.

The first of the wind blades struck Maple.

She took no damage, but it still sent her flying backward.

"Yikes!"

"Water Wall!"

Sally quickly threw up a barrier to buy them a few seconds, racing to Maple's side.

The knockback effect had flung Maple so far that Sally was outside the angel's protection.

And even Sally couldn't dodge her way through a carpet-bombing.

"Maple, Heavy Body!"

"Oh! Right! Heavy Body!"

Maple had almost forgotten her new skill, but she quickly activated it.

Now she couldn't move at all—but the wind blades couldn't knock her back. Sally quickly slipped into safety behind her.

"Hmm, but now we can't get close?"

"Bad luck meeting this thing in a one-way corridor. We've gotta do something about this knockback…"

"…How about…Heaven's Throne!"

Her gleaming white throne appeared.

And when Heavy Body ran out, Maple was knocked back—directly into her seat.

"Now it can't fling me anywhere!"

Her field of protection meant that even if a wind slice hit Sally, the knockback would hit Maple instead.

"I'd better tackle the cause. Maple, hit it once for me?"

"Roger! Deploy Barrels!"

Pillars rose from Maple's arms, aiming a pair of massive cannons at their enemy.

These fired dazzling laser beams, which knocked aside wind blades as they streamed toward the cloud monster. But the lasers were blocked by a wind barrier, which dispelled them before they could hit home.

"Hmm, I think I get it. This barrier only covers it from the front."

"Anything we can do about that?"

"I'll pull its focus, so you hit it when I do."

Sally put her daggers away and fired her webs at the wall, ready to climb it.

"Make sure you don't get hit, Sally!"

"Of course. I already figured out how to knock these blades away."

Both girls knew what they had to do.

Sally moved first, using her webs to pull herself up the wall.

"Ice Pillar! Fire Ball! Oboro, Flame Pillar!"

"Commence Assault!"

Sally was making footholds and knocking down wind blades, slipping through them toward their foe.

Maple was firing lasers, helping thin the incoming barrage.

It had caught them off guard, but if they worked together, they could handle this.

Sally came down the wall right behind the cloud and closed in, daggers swinging, wreathed in a blue aura.

Her blows were blocked by the wind barrier, but Sally didn't let up.

"Ice Pillar! Right Hand: Web! One Step in the Grave!"

And as the monster turned toward Sally, ready to bombard her—

Her webs shot to the top of a pillar, and the shoes Maple had given her let her step once on the air, letting her bound away.

"Aww, you should *never* have looked at me," Sally said.

Down the hall, there was a boom—and a column of flames billowed.

Maple came rocketing through the smoke, right past the monster.

The barrage of wind blades and the wind barrier were aimed to the front—now away from Maple.

"Commence Assault! How do you like that?!"

Full-bore lasers from point-blank range, and a shield that gobbled up everything it touched. The monster's HP was gone in the blink of an eye.

"And the finishing touch!"

Maple slammed her shield down one last time, and the monster vanished in a shower of light.

"Nice work, Maple. Good combo."

"Hmm! Thanks, Sally. Oh, hang on..."

After Maple dismissed her throne and her artillery, she brushed the soot off.

"Ugh, they don't have that much HP, but they're all as strong as your average field boss. And they're just hanging out in the halls of this place... Is it because we chose the hard one?"

"...I bet they're thinking the same thing," Sally said, shooting Maple a look.

"......? You've lost me. But let's keep moving! We don't want that thing respawning while we're still here."

"Good point. Let's bust through the back end."

They moved on. Sally kept on spotting traps and helping them slip past what monsters they could.

Down a monster, press on. Down another, press on.

And in time, Maple and Sally found themselves at the boss room.

They'd taken no damage, but all those fights meant Maple was out of Devour.

"Not bad for a first floor. Nothing using piercing damage."

"That was a relief! I hope the second floor is the same."

That type of attack alone made all the difference to her build.

Her defense was sky high, but she had very low HP—she would not last long if anything hit her one weakness.

"Mm. So we'd better hit this boss up and get that second floor open!"

"Yup. We've been playing awhile, so this is probably the last thing we do today?"

"Yeah, that sounds right."

And with that, they opened the doors and stepped inside.

Rough rock walls and a floor covered in a network of cracks.

There were many patches of sand, and the ground where they could easily walk was incredibly limited.

"……Sally."

"Hmm. Definitely coming from below."

No sooner had the words left Sally's mouth than the sand began swirling, and a dragon covered in sand-colored scales emerged from the ground below.

Red glowing eyes locked on to them, and an earsplitting roar shook the room.

"Maple!"

"Commence Assault!"

They both knew their roles by now. Sally broke into a run, and Maple started firing.

Bullets and lasers raced toward the dragon, ready to bring the pain.

But the dragon took one look at them and roared—and transparent crystals covered the surface of its body. All her attacks bounced right off!

"......! Superspeed!"

Sally turned into a blur, batting Maple's stray shots and ricocheting rounds aside with her daggers, ducking under the lasers before dancing back into range of Martyr's Devotion.

"Sorry, Sally!"

"Nope, don't sweat it. Maple, we should probably go in closer for a look-see."

"Yeah, roger."

Maple moved in front of Sally, covering her with shield and skill.

Martyr's Devotion couldn't do much against AOE piercing skills, so it was vital to keep her shield raised, too.

They hunkered down, waiting for the dragon to close. It dived back into the sand.

"Watch the ground, Maple!"

"Gotcha. Deploy Barrels!"

With a clunk, Maple's biggest guns came out. She pulled Sally close and belched smoke, flying up near the roof.

The dragon popped out where they'd been standing, but it couldn't reach them that high up. Sand and boulders rained down around it.

"As always, totally nuts...but badass."

"Down we go!"

Maple's flight was basically just blowing herself up, and it wasn't really great for landings.

So she simply let herself fall back down, with Sally on top. The impact broke all the weapons that had survived the explosion.

"How do we tackle this…? Hmm?"

Sally saw a black rock rolling on the ground. It was one of the stones that had come flying out when the dragon attacked from below.

As Sally tried to pull a thread through that thought, Maple yelled, "Sally! Something's coming! Pierce Guard!"

But her warning was drowned out by the dragon's breath attack—a violent torrent of sand.

The breath hit Maple's shield and launched them both backward. They went tumbling across the ground.

Maple's Pierce Guard had kicked in just in time, negating the attack's piercing damage, and Maple soaked the rest.

"Sorry, got lost in thought."

"No worries."

Another howl echoed—

—and then the black rocks scattered all around them *exploded*.

"Maple! That's it! We use those rocks to fight back!"

"……?"

"Throw 'em into its mouth when it readies the breath attack! If attacks from outside bounce off, the *inside's* its weak point!"

"Yeah? Okay then!"

It may have dominated the fight this far, but now they were ready to turn the tables.

They waited for the dragon to scatter those rocks again and then sprang into action.

"I'll keep it busy! Maple, you handle the rocks!"

"Got it!"

Sally slipped outside Martyr's Devotion, attacking the dragon.

Her blows all bounced off, but they were drawing aggro as intended; the dragon's talons and tail came after her in a flash.

But Sally could now run in three dimensions, and swings that big would never hit her.

Meanwhile, Maple gathered rocks in back.

"Heads up, breath coming," Sally said.

The dragon didn't make it easy for them. This time the breath attack struck in a horizontal pattern.

"Whew."

But all Sally needed was focus. She ran right up into the air, avoiding the breath's swipe.

When the roar of sand died down, she glanced back, searching— and Maple flew past her.

"Huh?"

Maple had a bunch of rocks wedged in her weaponry and was rocketing straight through the sandy air—

—right into the dragon's mouth.

"Heh-heh-heh... Now it's *our* turn! Full Deploy!"

The rocks she'd brought in with her all exploded, but that didn't damage *Maple*. The dragon tried to chew her up, but she was much harder than any mere rock. It could break her artillery guns, but those fangs never reached her HP.

"Hydra! Commence Assault!"

Stuck inside the dragon's mouth, Maple simply deployed her weapons again and started firing every cannon and laser and poison geyser she could.

The dragon thrashed like a wild thing but could not dislodge her.

Her weapons exploded rather frequently, but Maple was immune to explosions.

On the other hand, the dragon's HP bar was dropping steadily.

"Hngg…stay still! Augh!"

The dragon had tried to dive under the surface with Maple still trapped in its maw, but as its head went under, Maple shifted to Atrocity form and tore her way out of it.

It was all too easy.

The dragon's body lost shape and returned to the sand from which it had come.

Sally came jogging over the heap, searching for Maple.

Only Maple's head was above the surface. Giving Sally a plaintive look.

"…Need a tug?"

"Please."

Sally's final act on the first floor was to rescue Maple.

While the event was live, the admins had to monitor both the regular zones and the special-event map.

The room was filled with the sound of constant keystrokes.

"They're making short work of the highest difficulty…," one developer grumbled, glaring at his screen.

It showed the current floor and the number of people on it—even at the highest difficulty, there were already players on the third floor.

"Yeah…but we made all those bosses tricky enough that they won't exactly clear it overnight."

The speaker didn't even stop typing, clearly certain that anyone would get stuck eventually.

"Still, we could maybe up the difficulty a bit overall. People are making pretty short work of the second-hardest difficulty, too."

Players were exceeding expectations on all versions of the tower run. But this was partly because players capable of tackling the highest difficulty had decided to go one level lower.

"Well, it's only just getting started. What do you think? Should we take a peek at a boss room?"

"Let's see one on the hardest difficulty, then. Someone's just starting that fight."

"Give me a sec. Ooookay, up on-screen now."

"Hmm..."

The man closed his eyes, clearing his mind. Ready for anything. He shook his head and slowly opened his eyes.

And saw a girl in black armor and a girl decked out in blue.

Maple and Sally.

"Ah...mm. Welp. Can't hurt."

He'd been hoping to see *normal* play, but no such luck.

The dragon was going all out, and they seemed helpless against it.

"Tanky as ever. Still, this ain't a boss you can out-DPS."

"It does have piercing attacks, right?"

"With a clear and obvious windup. She can block if she knows it's coming."

Even as they spoke, the dragon's breath swallowed the girls up.

The man looked rather taken aback.

Sally hadn't even *tried* to dodge.

"She didn't evade? I mean, sure, no damage. But the force is still pretty intense..."

"Nothing new. Sally is under Maple's devotion. Still...hmm."

The man put his hand to his mouth, thinking.

Then his eyes went wide—just as Maple flew *into* the dragon's mouth.

"Why?"

"Well, the bombs—ack!"

A wave of virulent poison spilled out of the dragon's maw. Lasers gleamed in all directions, and the explosions were far too powerful to have come from those rocks alone. As the dragon tried to seek refuge underground, its body split apart, and a hideous monster clambered out.

"Or...not *just* them..."

"Inside... She went inside..."

"Where did we go so wrong?"

"The moment we let it open its mouth."

But if it kept its mouth closed, it would be more of a boulder than a dragon.

Then again, the design concept had basically been a moving boulder.

"Why did she just jump right in without even *trying* to throw the rocks?! I'm pretty sure we presented an obvious strategy!"

This was a natural question, but one nobody here could answer.

"The next boss doesn't open its mouth! It'll be okay. She can't... do *this* to it anyway."

"Show this to the others later. Especially whoever designed the dragon."

"Yeah..."

Tragedy was best shared—and the man who had made the proposal spoke from experience. He'd designed the second-stratum boss that Maple had pulverized.

He was not alone in his grief.

"Well, it won't work next time!"

"We say that every time!"

The two men decided it was time for their break.

And when they showed what had happened to the boss designer, his face crumpled, and his scream echoed throughout the office.

CHAPTER 11

Defense Build and the Tower's Second Floor

With the first floor cleared, Maple and Sally logged out, saving the second floor for later.

Once a boss was defeated, the system would save the progress and allow players to continue from the last floor they'd reached.

When they returned, Maple and Sally stepped onto the second floor and found both walls lined with shelves, all filled to the brim with books.

The shelves reached the ceiling, but the halls themselves were the same size as the floor below.

"A library?"

"Feels like one. Bet there's a lot of magic attacks…"

"And with the halls this cramped, I can't ride Syrup around!"

Giant Syrup was too big for most indoor areas.

Lots of things could be avoided if you were flying, but this event took that option off the table entirely.

"We'll just have to walk."

"Looks like it… That'll be slow going, though."

They figured it was best they get moving.

Books to the left of them, books to the right. Eventually they reached an intersection, the passage continuing straight ahead and branching to either side.

"......Left?"

"Left it is!"

They turned the corner, and a few steps later—

—a book shot off the shelf, hurtling toward them.

"......! Nuh-uh!"

Sally reacted in time, twisting herself out of the book's path and drawing a dagger to hit back.

The book-shaped monster sprayed red damage sparks but continued unerringly on its original trajectory.

The cover popped open, but unlike in real books, the pages were lined with *teeth*.

This alien-looking jaw bit down on Maple's face *hard*.

"Eek?! Hey...uh, Sally? I can't see! Get this thing off me!"

Maple was shaking her head, but the monster was firmly clamped on, and she couldn't dislodge it.

"Hang in there. Double Slash!"

The book was totally defenseless, so Sally had no problem landing a deadly combo.

These enemies clearly didn't have much HP, so it soon vanished in a puff of light.

"That was a shocker! I guess that *is* the kind of monster you'd find here."

"True. But that does make 'em hard to spot."

Sally could dodge even without prior warning, but she did have to stay on the alert.

No further books attacked. Maybe they had to cross specific points in the halls.

"Should I put Martyr's Devotion up?"

"Mm, please. We've already seen a bunch of wind magic and AOE attacks here."

Maple activated her angel form and chugged a potion to restore her HP.

Once those preparations were done, they headed off through the packed shelves once more.

"That book wasn't all that strong."

"Hard to say—it *might* have done a lot of damage? I just can't tell."

If Maple was on the receiving end, it was hard to gauge just how powerful a hit was.

The damage could be one or a thousand, it made no difference against her.

"…This floor's boss may be the same way. I'd at least expect a wide variety of attacks."

"I wonder if there's any info about it? Like in these books."

Maple reached for the shelf on her left and tried to pull a book from it. But they were fixed in place.

"No use! Oh well."

"But there might be something somewhere. We didn't explore half the first floor before we found the boss room, and it didn't really matter. Still, it can't hurt to keep an eye out."

"True!"

No sooner had the word left Maple's mouth than another book monster flew out.

This one loitered near the ceiling before dropping a lightning bolt.

The electric field spread out in all directions. There was a clap of thunder, and the passage lit up.

"What do you think, Sally? Should we get it?"

"Yeah, the strobing's getting to me."

Neither one of them seemed at all concerned about the potential danger.

Maple deployed her weapons and aimed the barrels at the book.

The first laser flash canceled the lightning bolt, and the second burned the book up.

Once again, the books proved no match for their relentless offense.

"Heh-heh-heh. No traps so far, either! This place is a breeze."

"You're making it one. Oh, three at once!"

Three glowing books were fluttering toward them. Sally gave Maple a look, and Maple knew just what to do.

"I got this!"

She aimed her weapons down the hall.

If they wanted to take Maple down, most monsters would need to venture inside her range.

They'd only just started this floor, and she could still use *all* her skills. That meant no random mob stood a chance.

Maple and Sally were making steady progress through the vast library.

But the place was a serious labyrinth, and every corridor looked exactly the same. It was impossible to tell if they were actually getting closer to the end.

Maple had gotten bored and swapped her gear for a change of pace. She was now in the green clothes she'd found on the sixth-stratum manor.

"How far are we?"

"Good question, We definitely walked a long way... Oh, here they come again."

Sally spotted several books flying their way down the darkened corridor.

Maple didn't need further prompting. She aimed her weapons.

"Heh! Commence Assault! Poltergeist!"

Maple's lasers fired, and then she waved her hands, changing their paths and burning up all the books.

The tower's difficulty being what it was, they weren't instantly vaporized, but multiple laser hits were definitely carving away at their HP.

Narrow corridors made this kind of fighting trivial.

"Gosh...that takes *skills*."

"If I move one at a time, it's easy! Like waving swords around!"

Maple demonstrated by swinging her arms.

Since the books were just coming head-on without bothering to make any evasive maneuvers, their HP just kept dropping, and soon they burst into shards of light.

"You are good at ranged attacks. This one's on the weird side but...*just* weird."

"Still, they don't do *that* much damage. And I'm not good enough to hit anything fast yet."

"Well, worth practicing. They should be pretty easy to hit with."

"Let's hope so... Oh, they're all dead already?"

Maple scanned the corridor ahead.

Sally did the same and found nothing moving.

"Flawless victory."

"Great! Let's keep moving."

*   *   *

Kicking the occasional book's spine, they continued ahead cautiously.

Each time they reached a corner, Sally carefully peered ahead, keeping them from as many fights as she could.

"Looks clear, Maple. Maple?"

"Well? Does this make me look smart?"

Sally turned to look. Maple had taken a pair of fake glasses out of her inventory and was peering through them at a thick tome.

There was a gap on the shelf beside her where the book had been.

"…Maybe if you hadn't asked?"

"Urp. You think? Mm. I guess I see that."

Maple flipped through the pages of the book.

Sally stepped closer, looking over her shoulder.

"All white? Nothing in it…"

"Should we write something? Augh!"

As Maple spoke, the book had suddenly turned to light, vanishing into thin air.

It reappeared in its original location.

"You can't take it with you…shame."

"If you could, *you* might find something weird to do with it. Right?" Sally said, giving Maple a pointed look.

Maple caught her drift and shifted uncomfortably.

"I don't…do that *all* the time. Or at the very least, it's not on purpose. Not always!"

"Yeah. That's…mostly accurate."

Sally was remembering a bunch of Maple's wilder exploits, and that left her nodding.

Many of them had been happy accidents.

She had just tried a thing and been surprised by the outcome.

"Anyway! Moving on!"

"Mm. No more enemies here...but it feels like it's getting darker."

Maple decided they needed light.

If she felt like it, she could easily add more shields or weapons—or a lantern.

Maple took the latter out of her inventory and lit up the passage.

"Sally...this lantern is usually brighter."

"......Could be one of *those* areas. Hard to be sure. Hmm... Fire Ball!"

Sally's spell flew off into the distance—and the flames were definitely smaller than usual.

"Looks like some spells and skills are weakened. Light and flame? You...should be good on offense, right?" she asked, mentally running down Maple's skill list.

Maple had a lot of skills that were light or dark, but none of her attack skills had names that made it seem like they'd be affected.

"Martyr's Devotion doesn't seem at all different... I wonder why not?"

She'd had that up the whole time, with no discernible changes.

"Maybe that'll change as we get farther in. I'll have to try not to get hit."

"You can do that, right?"

"You betcha. But if they use an AOE, make sure to get your shield up."

"Will do!"

They picked their way down the dimly lit passage, ready to squash any threats ahead of time.

*   *   *

Sally was in the lead, and Maple was bringing up the rear.

"Still haven't seen any—"

"S-Sally?!"

"Maple?"

Sally spun around.

Behind her, Maple's feet and weapon were totally immobilized, caught in the grasp of shadowy hands reaching up from the ground.

"You okay?"

"Uh…I just can't move—! Eep!"

"! Sorry."

Mid-sentence, several toothy books had chomped down on her.

Sally had deftly jumped out of the way, but Maple wasn't going anywhere.

"Sally! Get these off! I—I don't want this gear breaking!"

"Hold on, I'm working on it!"

Sally closed in and carved her way through one book.

They still weren't that tough, so she pried them all off before long.

"Now the hands…are gone? Huh…"

"My gear's still good, but I better get it fixed up later."

Maple switched back to her black armor, which boasted Destructive Growth.

Her gear's durability had taken a hit while Maple herself remained entirely unharmed.

However, Sally noticed something else amiss.

"Maple? Martyr's Devotion's gone."

"Huh? That's weird. Hmm…apparently, I can't use it for the next thirty minutes."

"So that attack sealed your skill? And the reason they only came after you...was either the angel form or because you were holding the lantern."

"But that didn't go out, so... Oh! But if they attack me again next time, we'll know they're targeting lights!"

"If it's just any old light source, Sword Dance makes me light up like a Christmas tree—but whatever the cause, with your defense, it shouldn't be a problem."

Their enemies could attack Maple all they liked.

It might ruin their plan to clear this tower without damage, but if these monsters turned out to be strong enough to get through her defense, Indomitable Guardian would prevent her going down instantly.

"Totally! I can defend against anything!"

"I'll spot pierce attacks for you, so be ready to use Pierce Guard."

"Mm, got it."

Maple hefted her shield confidently.

"But it looks like they're here already...," Sally muttered, far less sure of herself.

She was pointing into the darkened depths—where a shadowy figure stood.

The shadow had a single red eye, which was staring fixedly at the shelves.

"What now, Sally?"

"I don't even wanna go near it, but it's a one-way path. Uh...maybe on top of the bookcases? But maybe we should at least figure out its deal."

"Can you...get us up there?"

"Well, more quietly than your flight anyway. Wanna try?"

Maple was all for it, not wanting to fight more than they had to.

"Gimme a sec."

"No problem."

Sally prepped by wrapping Maple in her webs. Then she put two rings on, boosting her STR, and put down an ice pillar.

"Here we go."

"Huh?"

With Maple still attached, Sally began pulling on the strings—while running up the pillar and the wall to the ceiling.

Maple was yanked upward with incredible force.

"Oh...my...!"

Legs dangling, Sally pulled her all the way up.

Then they sneaked along the top of the shelves past the monster and dropped down a safe distance beyond.

"Whew, that was easier than I thought."

"I-it was amazing! You're like a ninja!"

"I bet we can find a use for that again somewhere. If it's cool with you, of course."

"It's a fun change of pace! Minty fresh."

"Not a thing you could ever do in real life. But that thing really doesn't budge, huh?"

Sally glanced back down the corridor, and the shadow was still standing there.

It wasn't moving at all. Sally watched it for a minute but couldn't detect any changes.

"Does it attack if we get close? We'll have to try that if we end up in a position where we can't find a way to slip past it."

"Yeah. Would be scary if they show up as adds in the boss

room—but if this is the only one, then we probably don't have to worry about that."

Unable to figure out how big a threat this was, they decided to avoid it for now.

"Okay, let's move out, Ma—"

"Sally! I'm caught again!"

The black hands had grabbed a hold of Maple once more.

This time Sally knocked the books aside before they could bite her, but as she did, she spotted something.

"Maple, gimme a sec!"

"Mm? Okay!" Maple said, trying to peel a book off with both hands.

Sally raced back to the monster they'd just skipped.

She'd spotted a blue glow around it, and hands reaching up from a spot on the floor.

"If I know what you do, there's no prob! Double Slash!"

Sally hit it once, and the monster soon melted into the floor.

"Oh, they let go! I'm free, Sally!"

The hands that had been on Maple's feet faded away.

Now they just had to get rid of the books, which were old hat at this point.

When that was over, Sally said, "I don't think we can actually kill that monster. It just ran away. Probably hiding somewhere until it pops back up, coming and going at regular intervals."

"Nothing we can do?"

"Plenty of paths we haven't taken; one of them might have a solution."

They'd certainly not been trying to map the place, so they might have missed it.

"Think it'll show up in the boss room?"

"It might. And that would be bad news."

"Then we'll just have to take the boss out quick!"

"Good idea. Whatever skills it tries to seal, if we win fast enough, it won't matter."

These two definitely had the skills to romper-stomp most bosses, so if anyone had been there with them, this exchange would likely not have engendered argument.

They moved on.

Maple got her skills sealed a few more times, but eventually they reached the boss room.

The expected big door loomed far overhead.

"About time!"

"Part of me wants to check the paths we didn't take…but that can wait. Your skills still sealed, Maple?"

"Hmm…they'll be back in twenty."

"Then best we wait for that. Better to be in peak condition!"

They sat down in front of the door, killing time with idle chatter.

Once all Maple's skills were available again, they charged through the door.

"No change in theme, huh?" Maple said, glancing around.

The room itself was large, but the walls were covered in shelves, crammed full of books.

Sally peered into the dimly lit depths—and a blue magic circle appeared in the air.

"Mm! Maple, incoming!"

"Got it! Let's start with Full Deploy!"

As they braced themselves, the boss appeared—a massive book, several yards wide.

Glowing blue, it lowered itself until it was hovering just above ground level.

"Early bird gets the bookworm! Commence Assault!"

Even as Maple fired her opening volley, the book's pages flipped to a drawing of a book on fire.

In response, red books shot off the shelves on either side, shooting fireballs.

"Maple, you take the right! I'll cover this side!"

"Got it!"

Sally sped off, deftly taking books out with skills and magic.

But as she did, the big book's pages flipped again—this time shadows appeared in the corners of the room.

Five of the monsters that had sealed Maple's skills.

"Ack! D-don't—!"

"Can't get 'em all!"

"Hng, in that case…Hydra! Saturating Chaos!"

Maple shot her poison dragon and monster after the bullets, trying to hit the boss with them before the skills got sealed.

But the pages flipped once more—and now a blue barrier appeared in front of it.

The barrier intercepted the bulk of Maple's attacks. After a short while, it shattered like glass, but it had done its job. The damage the boss took had been dramatically reduced.

"Sally, I didn't do much!"

"High-attack moves can backfire like that! Lemme try! Superspeed!"

"I'll work on the shadows!"

Sally put out an ice pillar, vaulting over Maple's lake of poison to the boss's side.

Maple started shooting the approaching shadows.

Some of the fireballs hit her, but they seemed to have no side effects.

"How's this?"

Leaving it to Maple to deal with the incoming attacks, Sally sailed over the boss, slashing away with both daggers.

Without the barrier page open, the book was not terribly tanky; she did a solid amount of damage to it.

"Nice! And again!"

She used her webs to launch herself—but the book's pages flipped, and a gust of wind emerged.

Sally was forced to extend her webs, yanking herself out of range.

"That was close! Oh, there's a knockback effect, too."

She spotted Maple flying away, slashed the boss a few more times, then raced over to her friend.

"I took a chunk off it."

"Nice one, Sally!"

"Still a long way to go. Next...?"

They looked toward the boss just as its pages flipped once more.

But this time, it opened to a blank page—nothing on it at all.

"...What? Blank?"

"! Maple! Dodge!" Sally yelped.

But it was too late—black chains spawned at her feet, binding Maple in place.

Sally feared this would seal some skills, so she did her best to free her, attacking one chain at a time until they broke.

"Hmm...this isn't sealing anything!" Maple said.

"Huh?"

"It's worse! They're *stealing* my skills!"

All of Maple's artillery had vanished.

"...*What?*"

Sally cut the last chain, but the boss's pages were already turning.

To a page bristling with artillery.

"Crap...!"

Sally's eyes went white—and multiple magic circles spawned, barrels reaching out of them like so many branches.

"! Maple, sorry! Right Hand: Web!"

"Huh? Yikes!"

Sally snared Maple and dragged her away, fleeing the boss room.

Maple was banged loudly against the floor, towed helplessly in Sally's wake.

"...Retreat! Retreat!" Maple wailed.

"Yup! I ain't up for fighting a fake Maple!"

They barely made it through the doors before the newly formed artillery started firing.

◆□◆□◆□◆□◆

Maple and Sally slammed the doors behind them and collapsed against them.

"Whew… Okay, let's review."

"Wh-what do we do, Sally?"

"I mean, that depends…what exactly did it steal?"

They had to figure that out first if they were to stand a chance against the boss's latest tactic.

Maple opened her stat menu and checked her skill list. She was missing Machine God, Saturating Chaos, Heaven's Throne, and Pandemonium.

"And Atrocity was part of Saturating Chaos, so…"

"Urp. Doesn't even matter if you've stuck it on your gear? And it only took the good stuff! Any time limits?"

"Doesn't look like it. A-are they not coming back?"

Maple looked very anxious.

"If we beat the boss…or maybe leave the floor? I think at worst, they'll come back once the event's over."

But that would mean giving up on clearing this tower. And they weren't about to do *that*.

"Hmm…well, there *is* a way…"

"Oh? What is it?" Maple perked up.

"Might have to abandon the no-damage idea, but we could try forcing Martyr's Devotion on it. If the boss tries using that skill, it'll basically be suicide. But…even if we do get it to steal the skill, no telling if it would actually voluntarily *use* it."

"And if it steals Absolute Defense, we're sunk!"

"Yeah…without your defense, Maple, you're, uh…"

Just a normal girl.

Maple with no offense *or* defense frankly wasn't much use in combat.

"Wait, Maple, how much is your VIT? Without skills?"

"Mm? Uh, lessee… I haven't really thought about it recently."

She flipped through her menus, checking her raw VIT.

"Um, just over two thousand."

"Huh."

Sally closed her eyes, saying nothing more.

"Should I be more specific?"

"No, that would be negligible. A rounding error."

She had already concluded that there was no point worrying about Maple's safety ever again.

Since Maple had no piercing skills herself, no matter *what* this boss stole, it could never actually hurt her.

"In that case, Maple, you just keep me safe. I definitely can't slip through that barrage."

"You got it! What else?"

"Just hang in there. Let that boss steal skills until it grabs Martyr's Devotion and uses it."

Sally had done pretty solid damage with Double Slash, so she didn't think this boss had much in the way of defense.

Absolute Defense and Fortress were both heavily dependent on your raw VIT stat, so even if it stole them, they could still pull this off.

"Okay! Once that happens, we hit it with everything we've got!"

Maple thrust a fist out in front, ready to lay down the punishment.

"Mm. I can also foresee a few other headaches that we should plan for. While we're still safe and have the chance to anyway."

"Then let's get strategizing!"

They huddled up and began throwing out ideas.

*　　*　　*

When they were pretty sure they had their bases covered, they rose to their feet.

"It's really all about my skills, huh?"

"Maple—all your skills are *exactly* the kind of thing bosses use. If we don't have clear-cut plans in mind, I would never make it."

Maple might be immune to all her own skills, but Sally was much more fragile.

She needed a plan for each and every one of them.

"You've put the short sword and shield away?"

"Yep, they're gone! If I lose Poison Nullification, even I'd be in trouble."

The idea was that if her black sword and shield were stowed in her inventory, the boss wouldn't be able to steal the skills on them. She'd replaced them with the white gear Iz had made for her.

But the book had already stolen the skill from her black armor, so she left that where it was.

This left her defense lower than they'd originally planned, but since there was a real risk of Bug Urn Curse kicking in, they really didn't want to risk offering up Hydra.

They also weren't sure just how effective Devour would be on Maple herself, so they figured better safe than sorry.

"We don't know the exact boss stats. This might nerf you, but if it can get past your nerfed defense, then that attack's so strong it would hurt *everyone*. No use worrying about that."

"True. I hope it works out!"

Maple looked up at the door, a little nervous.

"Maple, ready when you are."

"…All right. Here goes nothing!"

Maple slapped her cheeks and raised her shield.

Sally nodded and shoved the doors open. Both girls ran inside.

*   *   *

The boss had fully recovered its HP and was back to its initial phase, summoning the fireball books and the skill-sealing shadows.

"Okay, it isn't starting with it. Once it does try and steal your skills, check what it takes and let me know!"

"You betcha!"

And with that last reminder, Sally raced off.

Maple did her best to keep up.

"The early stages look like they're the same, so no worries yet."

Like the last time, Sally began carving chunks off the boss's HP.

Maple was mostly using Taunt to keep the fireball books focused on her, but she positioned herself so she could use Cover on Sally as needed.

"Hmm…it's been a while since I used Cover Move. I think this was the range… Maybe I'd better get a little closer."

Adjusting her position, Maple watched Sally slash away, one eye on her feet to avoid getting skills sealed.

Sally was going all out, trying to get the HP down before her focus wore out. It didn't take long for the boss's pages to turn to a stolen skill.

"Maple!"

"Cover Move! Cover!"

Sally leaped back, and Maple didn't miss a beat, warping directly in front of her.

A moment later, bullets started pounding her.

"As long as I'm watching, it's no problem!"

The sound of bullets bouncing off her was jaw-dropping.

"I guess not? Seems like it doesn't try and steal skills all *that* often."

Given what they'd seen so far, Sally decided to stick to Maple's back like glue, and they approached together.

"Ugh, so many!"

"I didn't have time to notice last time, but all the adds vanished when it flipped to this."

"Oh, so they did! That makes it easier. Sweet!"

As they got closer, the bullets started coming in from above, and Maple had to hold her shield like an umbrella, keeping Sally safe.

"Nobody but you could ever soak these, Maple."

"Heh-heh-heh! Attacks like this are nothing! It isn't even coming for my other skills!"

"Yeah. Hmm, if the steal is a onetime thing, I guess I'll just start fighting back like normal."

"I got your back!"

"Good. Here goes!"

Sally slipped out from behind Maple and hit the boss hard.

She'd said she couldn't slip through the barrage—but here she was knocking bullets out of her path with the flats of her daggers, not even breaking stride.

Maple kept pace with her, shield up, keeping the durability loss to a minimum.

"Double Slash!"

With Sally's Sword Dance aura active, the boss's HP went down quick.

Sally had several ice pillars around and was using them to keep herself out of the volley's path.

Maple could tell this must have taken a *lot* of practice.

"...Sally!"

"Don't worry, I see them!"

When its HP dropped far enough, the boss activated two more skills.

A pair of monsters crawled out of the ground.

Then the now-familiar chains wrapped around Maple once more, trying to steal yet more skills.

"Whoa...this was our plan! We meant this to happen!"

"Maple, the Predators are after you!"

She was all trussed up, making her a great target—the monsters surged toward her through the barrage.

One giant mouth closed around her legs and torso, the other around her head.

Maple closed her eyes, but then she realized she wasn't taking damage and slowly opened them again.

"G-gosh...I didn't know what it looked like *inside* them! All this time we've been fighting together, too."

She checked the skills she was losing.

"Bug Urn Curse...Fortress, and Martyr's Devotion! Oh, and Absolute Defense."

She might not be able to see far in front of her, but she could check her skill menu as per usual.

Sally confirmed she was still going strong, and Maple could hear the sounds of her spells and more ice pillars spawning.

"I'm gonna finish this while the Predators are still focusing on you!"

Sally bounced off another ice pillar and used her webs and invisible footholds to dance through the air. The boots Maple had given her gave her an added degree of precision that made it look like the spells were avoiding *her*. In no time flat, she was up against the boss, her daggers stabbing down.

"Cool, it used Martyr's Devotion! I've got more targets!"

Sally started flinging spells around, and each little book she hit racked up more damage to the boss itself.

"Going well! I think!"

Ascending, descending, focus at the max, slipping through any gap in the onslaught.

"And the finisher!"

Sally sheathed her daggers, balled her fist, kicked off a midair foothold, and accelerated.

"I've gotta free myself...uh...got it!"

Maple had her inventory open, and she found one of the bombs Iz had made.

She dropped it on the floor at her feet, and the incoming bullets caused a chain reaction.

"How's *that*?! I can attack even without skills!"

Maple might have her head inside a monster, but she still seemed smug. The raging fires snapped all the chains restraining her, but those pet monsters weren't letting go.

"...Y-you can let go anytime now?"

The Predators finally let go—less because of what she'd said and more because of the binding skill wearing off. They turned and headed toward Sally.

"Oh no you don't!"

Free, Maple quickly looked around—and saw a ton of little books spewing flames, water, wind blades, and stone bullets in all directions.

And the big book had white wings outstretched. The attacks were coming so fast, Maple couldn't even find Sally.

"Uh-oh?!" Maple said, getting worried.

She hustled toward the boss—and its HP dropped like a stone. It exploded in a shower of light.

"Howww?!"

"And done. Whew, that was exhausting."

Sally came striding through the shower of light, landing before her.

Maple ran over.

"Y-you beat it?!"

"Yup. Thankfully, it used Martyr's Devotion. And good thing it didn't try to heal."

"Aww, I wanted to fight, too! Those things bit me, and I couldn't even see!"

"Well, I pulled you into this game. Sometimes I've gotta show off a bit, too. Lemme show off sometimes! Still, it was a bit mean to just leave them stuck to you."

Sally looked a *little* guilty.

Maple thought for a second, and then her face lit up.

"Oh, I know! Since I took out the first-floor boss, we're even. What say we make it a contest? See who can beat the third-floor boss?"

Sally blinked at her.

"…Uh, I dunno if I can manage that…"

"Well, if you can't, then I've already won."

Maple grinned triumphantly.

And Sally wasn't about to take that lying down.

"You're on! Next time I'll back you up properly *and* take out the boss!"

"Then let's hit the third floor! The early bird…I said that already."

"No time like the present? I'm in."

At that, Maple turned and ran toward the stairs.

"Don't let yourself get carried away next time," Sally muttered, chasing after her.

The seventh event had only just begun.

And each girl was certain the next boss was *hers*.

AFTERWORD

If something prompted you to pick up Volume 6, nice to meet you. If you've been reading this whole time, I can't be more grateful. My name is Yuumikan.

It's because of you that we've come this far, and I must thank you again.

If the news of the manga and anime adaptions thrilled you, I couldn't be happier. I know how blessed I am, both by the people who've been helping out since the first volume and by the readers who keep buying new volumes.

The task before me is to keep the novels, manga, and anime all enjoyable in their own ways. Each of those is a monumental goal in its own right, and sometimes I look back and can't believe I've actually made it here.

If this has given you joy, I am glad I wrote it.
And for everyone enjoying it, I want to bring you more.
Thus, I, too, am looking forward to Volume 7 someday!

Yuumikan